THE NIGHT BEGINS

ABIGAIL F. TAYLOR

LUNA NOVELLA #15

Luna Press PUBLISHING

www.lunapresspublishing.com
ISBN-13: 978-1-915556-00-4

For Kate, Kelsey, and Meg, who read everything.

Contents

Chapter One

Mama lives alone on the hill.

The way I always heard it, she brought that axe down on Daddy. But, I figure, as long as I'm not on her shit list, there's no harm in dropping by for a visit.

It doesn't take long to get down to hill country, a few hours at most. It's an easy drive with long, lazy stretches where you don't have to check with a map. It gets trickier in the autumn when dust settles real quick-like and the shadows stretch long and wide, fingering all those doubts you ever had about the safety of the hills. Whether you've known the hills your whole life with a back-of-your-hand comfort or not, shadows distort the earth and remind you that everything you thought you knew was a lie.

Chapter Two

Nature has a way of creeping out of the concrete. I've always liked seeing little bits of ivy pushing its blue and purple veined flowers along the sides of buildings or dandelion tufts that take over the cracks in the sidewalks and the lip of older roads. It reminds me that everything breathes and fights to be seen. All ancient life, no matter how deeply burned and buried, comes back. I'm sure my obsession with urban structures suffocated by all things green and rooted has something to do with where I was born. I'm choked by the city, like it was a skin so tight and thin it couldn't be mine. Whenever I see a weed overcoming a manmade structure, it's like a sign from an old friend: *We're here when you need us. Just ask.*

All of Texas is pretty much like this. There's eons of tarmac and hectares of tall, toothy skyscrapers that trap in smog, painting everything in grey-blues, grey-browns and industrial orange against a backdrop of horns, shouts and an arthritic tangle of music pulsing out of open doors and windows. Then turn a corner and *WHAM!* Green! Overrun and outgrown, devouring every single bit of rust and iron, commanding the shape of the earth, choosing what is allowed to stay standing. A different kind of loud that enchants and devours the idea that the country is dull and silent. I believe that it has something to do with Nature's demand for reciprocity. Everything is a little give-and-take, but when people take too much, the comfort and convenience of modern living is repoed.

From what I remember, Mama's a lot like this. I try not to dwell on the evil she did, but she's grown out of this earth and Daddy took too much and too fast. He dried her out, so she hydrated in his blood. She's like the storm in a disaster movie and everyone else around her is the unsuspecting civilian. Either learn how to adapt or die.

In all the articles and transcripts I read that were open to the public, and what I can almost remember, Daddy wasn't abusive. Not in the normal sense of the word. That meant Mama didn't have a good enough motive to kill him. Her lawyer, of course, had tried to spin it in a way to make her look as innocent as possible. Daddy was starved for attention and wanted to take up all of hers. People said he talked big. Not loud or full of lies. Just big. Wide, sweeping statements, movements peppering stories or fantastic thoughts that rattled through his head and were spit out as they came.

I remember bedtimes with him seemed to outlast the night. It was never just one fairytale. It was an oral marathon that paused only to break down the etymology of words, which he never pronounced the right way because of his Blackland prairie accent. Any number of words sparked a tangent until everything he tried to say came out of his mouth in a stutter and the corners of his lips were gummy for water. All his thoughts crashed into each other like a beachside rainstorm. They were both natural disasters and our middle of nowhere house was hardly more than a teacup. Of course it cracked.

He didn't have an off switch. I remember that too. Mama needed him to turn off and he didn't know how. So she did it for him.

Sometimes, if I think real hard on the last week he was alive, I remember Daddy giving her the silent treatment or short, staccato sentences. It was as if he tried proving to her that he could be silent or that she would hate the looming quiet the way he did. His dark eyes burned something awful too. They were iron put to hot coals, pointing at her as she moved around, minding her own business and keeping up with the household chores. The gloom settled a creaking weight in the house. Mama said she never even noticed his quiet or thanked him for trying. Or, at least, she never did when I was in the room with them. That whole week, the loudest thing in our house was the outdated avocado wallpaper clashing with the orange linoleum floors.

There isn't much more about Daddy that I remember without prompting; what I do has been altered and manipulated by what I've stitched together through police reports when they spoke to our scant few neighbors about his 'general disposition', photographs that Aunt Lou keeps in a shoebox and pieces of me that don't belong to Mama: my laugh, my dark, iron-flat hair, the uneven shape of my nostrils. In fact, the only unadulterated memories I have are his tobacco-stained tongue and how he tasted the words (he was a champion eater of words) and his hands, sun-browned and stained from the charcoal he made at the back of the house, punctuating the stories he told.

Two weeks before he died, a cavity in his mouth finally chewed through and the tooth broke apart at the dinner table. He laughed so hard because it scared me something awful, and he said, "Human teeth always fall out."

He told me it broke because of all the soda he drank when Mama wasn't looking. Because of him, I don't even mix Sprite in my liquor. I know anything that isn't water can rot the teeth, but Daddy is the reason I've seen soda as an unholy poison.

I'm near enough to the highway exit to spark old memories. Luckenbach, population ten, is about thirteen miles from towns big enough to not have their zipcode officially retired. The only thing left worth mentioning is the general store that doubles as a post office. It used to be that everyone who lived in town had a mailbox posted at the end of main street and a man from Fredericksburg would come out with our mail two or three times a week. The boxes were lined up by the mouth of a drift fence, checkered between white and rust-red. I used to sit there, in the fickle, prickling weather, and wait for the school bus with the only other kid from Luckenbach. He said he'd moved from a place called Vikuspuri in West Delhi. Why that has stuck in my memory and not the kid's actual name, I can't say. People stopped using the boxes the summer before Aunt Lou took custody of me and I left this town, what my twelve-year-old brain though then, forever.

I'm grateful that the gas station is a straight shot off the highway. My Avalon is running on empty and there's no way it can make to the only other gas station, thirteen miles away in Fredericksburg. I nearly miss it because dusk settled in so fast, but the tin roof catches the sweep of my headlights. Once I see it, all the gooey chocolate feelings I can't name attach themselves to memories I can't place.

I slide my car, tan now from the hours of dusty travel, to the pump before stretching my legs and stepping inside the store. I want to get a snack, too, in case I have to commit myself to a slapdash dinner. She's not a very good cook and it's one of those things that I'd never forget. Religiously every Wednesday, she'd bake rock-hard cookies or Rice Krispie treats that were blackened from the broil because she didn't know they were a no-bake dessert. Daddy used to say every meal she made was like going to church, "All you get is a burnt offering or a bloody sacrifice." Mama sometimes laughed at that, but other times she'd slam the plates down and leave the room.

If I can get some snacks now, I can eat a little bit of whatever she's cooking so I don't hurt her feelings and have something to get the rotten flavour out of my mouth after she goes to bed.

For all the modernness of the gas pump, the building itself is steeped in the past. Most tiny and bucolic places take between twenty to fifty years to catch up to the world around them. Sunwashed brown clapboard sides and handworked benches for the old folks to sit while they wait for something interesting to pass by on the buzzing highway. Above the bench is a low awning that rat-a-tat-tats with the autumn rains and hailstorms. It looks like thin strips of metal are nailed down and replaced almost every year due to tornadoes, but the patchwork is almost hidden entirely by the ancient oak that bulged like a warty hand, threatening to crash down onto the left side the building. I bet if I look into the hollow in the centre of the trunk, I'd find it filled with a crow's treasure of gleaming buttons and brass toys.

A string of sleigh bells clang when I push open the wooden door and I'm hit with the welcoming and pungent smell of lentil and tarka dhal. I think of the little kid that stood at the bus stop and wonder if his family is still here and if they've taken over the gas station. Or is it someone else entirely? It's a hard guess to make. After all, with only ten people left to maintain a ghost town, I can't imagine any of them being a young family.

I take a minute to gather my surroundings. Behind the counter, a lean man looks away from the tiny, box television and offers me a polite, "Howdy!" He's in blue slacks, crisp white shirt and a turban so yellow it's like he kidnapped the early morning sun and wove it into the fabric.

We nod at each other and he watches me for a minute, one eyebrow bouncing, before he turns back to the TV. It's some old movie with the subtitles turned on. People are singing and dancing on top of a train. He pauses the tape to write in a blue moleskine notebook. Then he rewinds the tape a few seconds and presses play.

Something about him, maybe how stiff and triangular the collar of his shirt is, reminds me of the kid I used to sit by while waiting for the school bus. Maybe it is him and that's why he stared at me? I'm embarrassed that details of my childhood keep wet-sand slipping. I couldn't even recall who the bus driver was or what he – she? – looked like.

The only other person in the store is a fat guy, pale blond hair sprinting from a crinkled forehead. I can't decide if he's ancient or just a middle-aged rancher and work's just that rough on the body. In front of him rice and potatoes steam out of a blue and white lace patterned ceramic bowl. We ignore each other.

My boots smack gently against the tile as I wind past two short wooden shelves with DVDs and VHS tapes of Bollywood movies and blockbuster hits from the nineties. The only new and fresh items are the snacks and sugary drinks lining the back wall. On my way to the coolers, I nearly knock into a rickety metal lazy Susan with bumper stickers. All of them read, *Everybody's Somebody in Luckenbach!* And I'm tempted to buy one for my hand-me-down car. "See?" I can boast to Aunt Lou, "I'm a somebody!"

In the end, I lose the nerve. Aunt Lou abhors displays of any kind. A sticker slapped on a car that she's finally paid off would earn me a whooping. I may be technically an adult, but she's still capable of forcing me to pick my own switch from the yard. So I only take a glass bottle of Snapple Peach Tea and a bag of pretzels to the counter. The cashier smiles again and pauses the movie again.

"What's that?" I ask, pointing to the beautiful woman. Her hips and arms frozen in the sway of the train as it disappears into a rocky tunnel.

"Dil Se. This is the Chaiyya Chaiyya bit," the man answers. I can see the skin under his beard darken. He's pretty when he blushes. "It's the song they used in Moulin Rouge."

"Oh," I say, with no clue what he's talking about. Aunt Lou didn't allow those types of movies in the house.

"I still have to watch parts with the subtitles, but I'm learning!" He shuffles my items around, checking the price stickers and tapping the numbers into the computer. His thumb brushes the dampness off my Snapple bottle and, for a brief moment, I wonder if he has calluses. I push the thought aside. This man has a distinct hill country accent and that means he was most likely born and bred here. Which means he knows exactly who I am, even if he doesn't know my face. Totally off limits. Honest to God, nothing can ruin a date faster than admitting you're related to a murderer. Even worse when the date is a True Crime junkie. Still, it's hard to play the stony and detached stranger to his chicklet white smile.

He asks, "You get everything you need? I got tandoori

chicken made fresh this afternoon. Or jeera aloo if you're a veggie?"

I wave away the offers. His sweetness is all the more reason I better end any hope of a fling now. "Just these. Oh, do you have any mail for Althea Mills?"

"Ah," he leans on his strong arms and the dark hairs of his moustache turn up like the whiskers of a satisfied cat. "Darcy. I thought it was you!"

The old man hunched at the table, grunts, "You look like her."

"Who? Althea?" asks the cashier.

"No. Dummy! Her kid."

"She just said she was Darcy."

"And I said what I said." The old man clacks his plastic spork against his bowl, his nose pink and runny from the spices in the dish.

The other man rolls his eyes in a forgiving way. "Nothing for Althea. Not Amazon or anything. I couldn't give it to y'all, anyway."

"Why not?"

"Cuz you aren't Althea, are you?" He leans in conspiratorially and stage whispers. "It's against the law."

"Oh," I hadn't thought of that. It used to be I could walk down to this store and buy Daddy his tins of long cut Grizzly without anyone thinking about the law.

The cashier smiles bigger and tells me my total, then slips me a card with the store's number. "You call me if you need anything. String. Hammer and nails. Some good dinner. It's Gagandeep, by the way. If we're friends. 'Hey you' if we aren't."

I nod, certain that the heat in my neck and cheeks is visible to him, and I can't quite look in his eyes. There's just some people too beautiful to be allowed. The longer you stand near them, the more you're burned by their light. I'm sure I'll see him plenty this week, since he's the only place in spitting distance. I'm so distracted by him, and by the old man glaring and sniffling over his food, that the cashier's name fell right out my ear. I don't think I could have pronounced it right on the first go, anyway. "Can you say it again?" I ask in a small voice.

"Hey you," he says slowly. Smiling. Always smiling.

I try to smile through my prickling shame. Where was that cool, educated girl I am with the coffee shop boys next to the university library? My attempt to push any interest away with my own name has utterly failed. I wonder if he's one of those true crime people. "But I thought we were friends."

"Oh, alright!" He plays like he's waving the white flag at the end of a battle. "You can call me Gagandeep. Need a receipt?"

"No thanks." I start to step back but he's looking at me with some quiet expectation. A little cough escapes and I manage, "Goodnight, Gagandeep."

"Goodnight, Darcy. Drive safe."

"Pah!" says the old man as the bells above the door clang with my swift exit.

Whatever meet-cute fantasy I just had boils my brains the rest of the drive. I roll down my window to catch the crisp autumn night. My version of a cold shower. I bet my roommates and half the dorm are already down by the beach, digging a fire pit in the sand. Someone is wearing an oversized University sweater that doesn't belong to them in a desperate attempt to stake claims, to start a fling of their own. Someone else is rolling a joint, passing a beer, daring us to dive into the cold water. Another, a movie nerd probably, follows the dare up with a tone-deaf take on the Jaws theme music. That could be me. I should be there, trying to get on with my life instead of picking at old, greening scabs.

I pass a rotting signpost and my headlights catch the faded white paint: Luckenbach Pop 300. That was certainly a lie when I lived here, never mind now. It's just a forgotten relic of the past, choked out by Nature taking what she's due. I can't imagine Luckenbach ever having so many people. It's such a strange thing, too, that number. My suburban graduating class had nearly six hundred students, and I'd be hard pressed to give you the names of anyone out of my friend circle. But for a town? That's hardly anything at all. Luckenbach really is a place where everyone knows your business.

At least with a population in the hundreds, Mama might have been able to pass off her murder as a misunderstanding. "Me? Murder John? What a thing! That's pure gossip down at the salon and you know it just as good as I do." Unfortunately for her, and for me, she killed Daddy when there were hardly a handful of people living here and not a cable box between them.

As I turn off the main road, another memory strikes. A young Angus bull got loose and trampled all over the drift fence and the checkerboard mailboxes. By the time Gagandeep and I were dropped off at the end of the school day, the bull was grazing in the field. Leaflets and letters cluttered the street, torn and drifting like snow. I'd only ever seen snow in the movies and I danced through the bits of paper catching in the lazy summer breeze until Mama showed up and made me quit.

After that, all anyone did was blame the bull for making the town unincorporated. If it weren't for him, they'd be able to mail in their votes and keep the tax money flowing into Luckenbach. Soon enough, it wasn't just the town losing its identity on a map, it was every little problem. "Half my eggs broke because I hit a pothole in the street. All account of that no good bull! Bull *shit*!"

A town this small doesn't have a place in the modern world. It belongs in fairytales. And Gagandeep is the temptation that turns the hero's focus. Or is he the hero and I'm the one to lead him astray? After all, I'm the intruder. I'm the one with monsters hiding in the closet. I'm the one that burst into Luckenbach and questioned its existence. If this were a movie, I'd be the awful warning and Gagandeep would be the young knight who had to remain steadfast and bold in spite of the dangers. Hell, he even had the crusty, old advisor sitting by his side.

For all its abandonment, there is something enchanting about the backroads of Texas and zipping through the numerous forgotten places. On the surface, it's simply the grace that comes with getting off the highway. (I swear that 35 has been under construction since 1846 and traffic has been backed up since then). Sometimes it seems like the same cars have been stuck there just as long because of how slow they move, like every single one of them is wearing a fancier, shiny skin but the insides are rusted and worn down so that the only option they have left is to chug along in a desperate bid not to break down and get buried in the construction. Once you can finally snake your way off of it, your blood winds down and you can shake off all the idiot behaviour you're still carrying with you miles after the bad driving has already happened, the landscape really opens its lungs to you.

I had an English teacher in the fifth grade that told us,

"When you tell a story, you have to take the *you* out of it! Second Person narration makes it look like you're telling the reader how to think, and it distances you from what you're trying to tell."

She means that I ought to say, "Once *my* blood winds down," and, "The landscape really opens its lungs to *me*". Now, I don't know what kind of candy and sunshine life she had, but she definitely wasn't the type of person that understood some people want distance put between them and what they want to talk about.

It feels safer imagining my past as a Choose Your Own Adventure story. It's not that I ever did anything interesting. Up to this point, my life's pages have always consisted of hitting a dead end and having to flip back to an earlier point so I can hurry up and get nowhere fast. I've always been the observer, never the star of the show. Remarkable doesn't exist when you're forced to wait in the wings while everyone else gets a spotlight.

Remarkable and good are not the same thing. Spotlights, too, are not always something to be admired. Mama didn't do good when she cleaved Daddy's brains in half, *but* it was remarkable. The spotlight on her lasted a while too. It was so bright that it washed out all the dark and hidden corners of our country bumpkin existence. That light even fanned itself onto me long enough to push me into foster care until Aunt Lou saw it as an act Christian charity to whisk me away to a city so big I became invisible again. Maybe the invisibility is what got me thinking that my childhood happened to another little girl. Or, better yet, it happened in a book that I shouldn't have been reading or a television show that was meant for grownups.

It's only when I start pushing my Avalon up the hill and the radio cuts out that I realise I've let my thoughts meander too far. The road hypnotised me and I'm not certain how far away I am from the house. I fiddle with the radio but it only catches the blast of Flo Rida's *Whistle Song* before it all goes static again. That's how I know I'm close. I could never get a good signal on my Mushu radio clock. I'd saved hundreds of cereal box tops just to get that clock sent to me in the mail. Tragically, it never worked the way it was supposed to. Then again, it was possible that, since it was a toy, it was never meant to pick up a radio signal.

Mama's porch light winks at the end of the twisting lane and I lean forward, squinting as I pass through a patch of fog. At first, thinking it's my windshield, I push my hand against the glass. Now that I know it's not me, I turn off the radio to fully focus. It's so dense that the lick of flame from the porch's lamp disappears. I slow the Avalon to a crawl until I break through the other side and scream. I slam on my brakes with both feet as a massive aoudad turns its shaggy head to me. Its eyes are yellow and silver in the headlights. He gives me a disapproving gaze before plodding on. I wait, watching him to clear the road. Other aoudads bounce over the scrub and kick up the red dirt.

My heart is in my throat by the time I pull up to Mama's gate. She stands by the kerosene lamp, hand cupped around her beady eyes as she peers down at my tan car, a shining stain in the darkness. Her attention digs into the back of my neck, watching as I pull open the squeaking gate and close it again before driving the rest of the way to her front door.

"Darcy? Is that you?" I don't remember her voice sounding so brittly patched.

"Who else?" I ask, grabbing my overnight pack from the passenger seat.

"You made it." She doesn't step down from the porch. "I was worried. It's getting late."

"Late? It's not even seven."

"Late. Dark. Same difference. You found it okay?"

I tell her about the fog and the aoudads, and she nods and pinches my fleshy elbow as she guides me into the house. "Funny stuff happens on the hill sometimes. It's just how it is. Take your shoes off. I've only just finished waxing the floors."

She points to wilted newspaper on the left side of the door. An axe leans against the wall. Its handle is smoothed down and polished raw by decades of use. Is it *The* axe? I want to ask her this but Mama's gone into the dark yawn of the house and I hug myself against the growing chill. The wind whispers through the trees, laughing at me. It is a stupid question. *The* axe is probably locked in an evidence room below the courthouse. I kneel down and take off my shoes. The skin on my neck prickles and I'm struck with the creepy thought that something followed me here and is watching with shining eyes.

Chapter Three

"Put your bag in your room. I'll get dinner going!" Mama's scratching voice calls from the kitchen. It's the only room that has a lamp. The rest of the house is thrown into the dark pitch of a dead fire. From the hollow mouth of the kitchen, gold-orange light splashes across the wall of the stairs and a cheese grater drags across my stomach. The avocado wallpaper is torn off from the hip down and a wedge of the orange carpet is cut out, revealing the dusty floorboards beneath. Daddy was killed in the hall. His head landed with a wet smack against the bannister and Mama told me to go to my room. She wasn't holding anything then but she had the snap of flint catching in her dark eyes.

I decide to not fiddle with the hall lights, since I don't want to see more of the crime scene than I already have. It's not difficult to make my way, half blind, to my old bedroom. It was meant to be a solarium when the house was first built in the eighteen hundreds. The door is frosted blue glass and, when I was little, I decorated it with thin coloured papers and art projects from school. It's the room just before the stairs and all the warm western sun bakes it during the summertime. The windows are so big and wide it made sneaking out of the house easy. I never did, not really. Where would I sneak off to? All my class friends, besides Gagandeep, lived more than twenty miles in the other direction. Sometimes the backs of my legs or the hooks of my arms would tingle and ache from growing and I had trouble sleeping at night. I would hang my feet out the window and trail my toes in the damp, tall grass while I picked at the fuzzy brown spots of hair that had begun to grow around my calves and knees, waiting for the pain to pass. The windows were how I escaped the house the night Daddy died. It hits me in small flashes, like smudges of paint but I'm standing too close to the canvas to really see my memories and understand them.

As I push open one of the glass doors, an old bit of construction paper flutters to my feet. I step over it and sling my pink quilted travel bag onto the small bed. Then I pick up the paper and set it down on the nightstand. Mama's kept this stuff so long, I don't think she'd want me throwing it away without her knowing. When I snap my knuckles against the light switch, a naked bulb in the centre of the room hisses and clicks but remains off. I shuffle around the boxes stored in here to the curtains, nicotine-yellow and heavy, to push them open so I can use the moonlight to search for a flashlight or a spare bulb. It looks like Mama has turned my room into a sewing area but has kept most of the kid stuff if I ever decided to come back and reverse time. There are a dozen boxes, mismatched and awkwardly stacked against the closet's slatted door, rendering it useless. I hate not having a proper place to put my clothes when I travel. I vaguely remember the long nights I used to stare at the light creeping out the closet, hoping it was enough to keep the monsters away like Daddy said. Mama always said light brought monsters in, like moths. I was never sure who to believe.

The iron daybed is so much smaller than I remembered. A thin mattress, with thin pink paisley sheets, has lumpy coils that gave a surprising shout when I slung my bag onto it. The only pillow left on the bed is square and puffy and I'm not sure if it's a pastel yellow or just stained from all the nicotine. I don't know if I'd be able to sleep in this room. This house. I realise it was a mistake to come here. All the splinters inside of me that I tried to patch up were surfacing again. I wasn't ready. I should have seen the school therapist before making a decision this big.

I press my forehead against the window, considering the benefits of having the crisp, clean air clear out the musty smell of my old room. An itch of intuition stops me from raising the latch. There's something breathing out there.

I can feel it.

It isn't the normal night creatures; the owls and skunks, the wild boars rutting in the undergrowth. Not the coyotes. They prefer their distance. There's something sinister and I can't convince myself that it's just all my detached memories and fears of this old house. Out by the treeline, there's a lump disrupting the silhouette of trees. I wait for it to move but, as my eyes adjust, I remember. It's Daddy's coal burner. If it were morning, I'd see only the bald remains of timber, culm and straw that hadn't been picked away by the rodents and birds. Daddy always told me to never go near it. It was too dangerous. I might fall in the chimney. The truth is that I never wanted to, anyway. He made charcoal at dusk or dawn, whenever the light was weakest. The air stank like burnt hair or one of Mama's dinners. Whenever it was a burning day, the world went silent. All the crickets and cicadas found another place to sing, the coyotes and owls went further into the woods to hunt. I can't imagine Mama using it. She never said anything and I forgot Daddy made charcoal until this moment. There was something else attached to the burner too. A poem he used to recite or one of his platitudes.

"Marco? Polo?" Mama calls out to me.

"That's not how the game works!" I shout back. Unable to find a flashlight or another bulb, I close the curtains. They slice across the rod, like knives sharpening. Or is that Mama in the other room, making dinner? I didn't even think about the light on my phone, but I don't care enough now to put in the effort.

"How would I know?" she replies. "I've never had a swimming pool."

I join her in the kitchen, trailing my fingers against the peeling wallpaper to help guide me. It's breezy outside and that makes the walls groan and crackle until they mimic the sound of someone walking around upstairs. It's not really a two-storey house. It's only a loft converted into a 'master suite' and the only other room is a tiny attic space overrun with raccoons.

"Mama, the lights don't work in my room."

She leans against the blue tiled counter, Virginia Slim pressed to the side of her cheek, like the button end of a Morse code wand. The lines around her thick lips pucker. They used to not be so visible, but now they creep toward the tender folds of her nostrils. Rivers, ivy and craggy marks on the body as the skin loosens. Nature takes back everything, somehow. "What?"

"The lights don't work in my room."

"Why would they?" She shrugs a plucked eyebrow and inhales on her cigarette. "Maybe in the morning we can put a bulb in."

"Maybe?"

"It gets enough light in the day." She rolls her head over her shoulders and looks at the round table.

I look at it and there's only a kerosene lamp, a twin of the one sitting beside her. It's prettier than the one hanging off the porch. This one has a copper well with a curling handle and peonies ornately painted against the curving sides. The fluted glass is blackened and stained. Does she only use these lamps? I'm tempted to run through the house and flick the switches mounted on the walls to find out.

"What is–"

"Electricity is a scam, and it's just me in the house," she says in an angry rush. "What do I need all those lights for?"

"I could help pay–" I start to suggest but she's cut me off with a smoky wave of her hand.

"Well? You gonna set the table or are we eating with our hands?" The ashes of the cigarette inch toward the mannish curve of her knuckles. "I'm making pancakes."

"Oh." I shift over to the cabinet closest to me and open it. It's full of beans, tomato paste and Spam.

Mama clicks her tongue against the roof of her mouth and gestures to the area next to the refrigerator. So. She's not against electricity, just lights? Aunt Lou liked to say that it was a waste of time to argue with crazy. So, I don't. I just do as Mama says.

She shakes a can of oil and sprays down a flat griddle she's just plugged into the outlet next to the sink. "Dishes are in there. Flatware is in that drawer with the knob."

The plates are plastic, the kind found only at the Dollar Tree, with pretty splotches of colour to make them look a little bit better than what they really are. A webbing of cracks spreads out of the centre of each plate. I think I'll get her a nice set for the new place, unless she has a nice set that's packed and these are just temporary? When I called her last week, for the first time in seven years, she told me she was downsizing and could use help with the move. I'm still not sure what that means or what she needs.

I collect the forks and knives, also thick plastic. I think maybe she doesn't have anything fancy. Ever. I don't remember what we used when we were a happy family. Were we? We must have been for a little while. After all, most awful endings start out in a good place.

"I met the guy that works at the general store," I try to make conversation. "The gas station? Gagandeep."

"He's a silly boy," Mama says, ladling runny batter onto the griddle. Flecks of ash fall from her cigarette and into the mix. "He wants to be a model."

"Like Waris Ahluwalia?" I ask, opening the refrigerator. There's only a few packets of fast food sauces and a bottle of out of date tartare spread. I'm proud of myself for not stumbling on the name.

"Who?" Mama, almost irritated, adds, "Drinks are in the pantry."

The pantry is just a floor-length cabinet that uses the wall as one of its sides. There's a stack of Dr. Slice, which I haven't seen on any store shelf in years. I go for the jug of water and crack it open before searching for the plastic glasses. There's two of them with kittens painted on the lip. *Hang in there.*

"Waris Ahluwalia," I pronounce it *ha-loo-wa-wa* and I'm pretty sure that's wrong but at least I sound confidant. "The one that was in all those Wes Anderson movies. All the movies that are, uhm, quick talking and have a lot of pastels."

"The OCD movies. I've seen the one about the man in the submarine." She nods. "I didn't like it."

"He was in that too!" My smile pulls at the dead skin on my bottom lip. I didn't think we would have something in common to talk about, and I'd worried that my week with her would be stilted and empty of any shared interests.

"Oh him." She smacks the first two pancakes on a paper towel. "The one with the hat and the beard. Silly boy."

I'm not sure who she's talking about. So I quietly fill up the cups with water and set them above the knives on the table. Mama carries the paper towel by its ends and the steam of the pancakes soaks through the bottom. At any moment they're going to drop on the floor and I don't know Mama well enough to know how she'll react. She plops them onto the table before the paper tears in half. "Ta-da!"

"Was he the one I used to sit at the bus stop with?" I spear a pancake. The outer parts are completely black but the centre is gooey and a thimble worth of dough sludged out where my fork has poked it.

"Who? Waris Alulu?" Mama's gone to get duck sauce from the fridge and drizzles it on her own pancake. She cracks open a can of Dr. Slice and drinks it warm. The nub of her Virginia Slim wiggles between her knuckles and it's gone out but she hasn't thrown it away.

I roll my eyes. "No. Gagandeep."

I wedge a triangle cut into my own mouth, making a game of how much I can chew without actually tasting. It has the distinct, slick and waxy flavour of reused lard. She has an old coffee tin on the stove where she pours leftover bacon grease, but there's also a fresh can of Crisco sitting between the stove and the deep kitchen sink. I can't even taste sugar or flour, only the goo fried into a round shape.

"Oh," she sighs. "They all look the same, don't they?"

"Mama!"

"What?" she looks at me with a curious tilt of her head. "I'm sure they think the same about us. I suppose. Yes. I can't think of any other immigrant kid that lived here." She chews happily and dabs her mouth with a McDonald's napkin. A stain of her lipstick, red as her stiff curls, trails on the edge of the brown napkin. My shoulders curl with how much it looks like the stripped down wallpaper behind me, breathing against my neck. Pulsing with Daddy's blood. Mama doesn't notice, her woody eyes on her plate. "He still lives on the other side of the hill with his parents. Did you see how the road split off? They've always lived there."

"I didn't." I cut more pancake. Maybe the smaller cuts will make it look like I ate more. "Is it where the fog bank was?"

"It could be." She moves her loaded fork through the puddle of duck sauce. "I wasn't in the car, was I? How can I say for sure?"

"I don't know. Maybe the fog catches in the same area every time?" I suggested with a bite. I don't like how she pushes at me like this, like it's my fault for making conversation and I should know about things that I've never experienced before. Like it's my fault my home is foreign to me.

Mama shrugs and speaks around a full mouth. "Fog is fog. Eat your dinner. We've got work."

But fog isn't fog. I know this. She knows this.

Daddy used to talk all the time about the fog. "It brings in The Good Neighbors, so mind yourself. Never whistle in the woods at night. Never step through a ring of mushrooms. Never let them know you're here. Why's that? Because, if they like the look of you, they'll take you for their own and you'll never come back. Sometimes them Folk take a baby just to torment the mothers, replacing it with a kid that's not all right."

Thanks to my poetry and short stories class last semester, I learned that Changelings were the only explanation given to parents whose children were born with neurodiversities. It came up in our discussion of Yeats' poem 'The Stolen Child' and it was the only time I actively participated. I'd been really excited to already know something and eager to share my insight. Daddy told me all the important information of how to keep safe, why babies are taken and how they come in with the fog. My hereditary superstitions received only a slight, sympathetic laugh from the classmates and a lip twitch from my professor, like she was only humouring me. I never lifted my hand up again or answered a question that wasn't on a test paper.

I'm not much for poetry. I don't know how to read past the fancy turns and find meaning between the lines, always searching for what the poet really meant to say. Why wouldn't they just say it? Why does a red wheelbarrow have to mean something more than what it is? Why does a stolen child have to be a symbol for some greater meaning of religion or innocence or whatever? I barely passed that class and maybe I would have done better if I could understand poetry was all fog.

After dinner, we leave the dishes in the sink and the hard plastic thuds against the metal base. *Ka-thud*. Like a wounded heart. I turn on the faucet but Mama reaches across from me and shuts it off quick. "Pipes make too much noise coming in from the well. We'll do it in the morning."

She picks up the kerosene lamp and cups her hand around the light as she walks from the kitchen and down the hall. I hesitate at the spot where Daddy had been killed. To walk over the space feels sacrilegious, but Mama passes over it like the space has only ever occupied a dust bunny. What am I scared of? It's not like the stains and shadows will suddenly rise out of the floorboards and wrap around my ankles. Knowing that doesn't stop me from hugging the opposite wall and tiptoeing along the edge.

"Did you get lost?" Mama laughs, standing over a stack of newspapers and flattened boxes. The lamp is on the table and the curtains drawn so that the swelling orange glow of fire doesn't creep out into the lawn.

"Sorry." I don't want her knowing that the house scares me, that I'm a little kid who can't help her mom when she needs it. "I was just making sure the grease was covered."

"Thank you kindly," she picks up one of the boxes and folded the base, then held it between her knees to tape it shut. "You coulda brought me a coke."

"I can get one now."

"Don't bother. We're here now." She spins the box in her hands and sets it on the coffee table. "We've got to wrap these up. One box for pictures and the rest for everything else."

The living room hasn't changed since before I was born. The wine stain red carpet matches the chunky stripes in the wallpaper that separates strips of pungent red roses and green, stabbing thorns. The green and ivy drapes are stained with nicotine. I can't tell at first, because the yellow is in even strokes. Then I take down the first picture, a watercolour of a rust and white spaniel, resale sticker still stuck to the glass plate, and I see the patch left behind in the wall. The more pictures we take down, the more square and oval patterns revealing the stunning white, green and red of the original wallpaper. All the faded yellow I thought was part of the colour palette was really the residue of Mama's habit. If new people buy this house, will they redecorate or will they bulldoze the place and be done with all the stains another life left behind?

"Here." Mama waves a stack of old newspaper at me. "Make sure you have the frames facing each other."

She doesn't have any photos of me, Daddy, or her. The only thing that nods to any hint of family is one of those big frames that have all different shapes cut into it so wallet-sized pictures that dated before 1950 can be wiggled into place. They're all Daddy's side of the family. I remember asking for photos when I was in the third grade and my homework was to make a family tree. Mama said she lost all her family pictures in a flood when she was a child. Daddy gave her a strained look but didn't push her about it, and I knew better than to ask twice.

"You gonna move back to Baytown?" I ask, setting the giant frame aside. It's too big for a box. Maybe all this nostalgia will finally get her talking about that side of the family and all those people I've never met.

"Why should I? Nothing good comes from your past." She pauses and lights another Virginia Slim. I can taste the menthol in the air now that I'm paying attention. She drew in hard on the cigarette and crackling of burning paper mixed into the creaking of the house. "I was thinking…" the ash drifts to the floor, leaving tiny tracks of snow. "Maybe I could move up north a bit. Closer to you?"

"Sure!" It comes out in a squeak. I never thought that she would want me so close. She never fought for my custody. "If that's what you want."

"Why wouldn't I want that?" she asks, sucking on the Virginia Slim. She places her small, puffy hands on her back and stares at the bookshelf stuffed with Precious Moments figurines. "Let's just do the first row and then turn it in for the night."

My arms flop down to my side. I don't know why I was expecting a hug, but I guess I handled the information wrong. She didn't even look at me when she told me she wanted to move closer to me instead of further away. She hands me a figurine with a little towheaded kid sitting in a teacup with a bunch of puppies. *God Loveth a Cheerful Giver* is scrawled in gold letters. "Clean off the dust before it's wrapped," she smiles and looks me in the eye now. "We don't want to bring old skin with us."

Chapter Four

We work until eleven scrubbing all the nooks of the figurines and gently wrapping them in newspaper. I never knew a person could have so many of one thing. My roommate has a shoebox full of bottle caps she finds interesting but there's not more than twenty in there. If she keeps collecting them until she's Mama's age maybe she'll have a whole closet of shoeboxes, but I just can't see that happening. I don't know how anyone can hold onto mindless stuff for such a long time.

My shoulders and neck are sore and the tips of my fingers are smudged with ink. I really want to take a shower but Mama insists we go to bed. "This close to the witching hour? Best we tuck in and not move around, making so much racket."

It's her house and, even if I believe she's acting a little 'old world' crazy, I can't do anything but consent to it. Who knows what might happen if she sees me roll my eyes about her superstitions? She could start lecturing me on Baba Yaga or to be wary of men whose eyebrows meet in the middle. I secretly suspect she's just using an excuse to hide the fact that she's scared of the dark and the noises that bounce inside of it. I'm not sure why that is but, while we worked, we barely spoke. There was only the hiss of the lamp and crickets and bullfrogs putting on a performance in the wide, sweeping yard.

Mama picks up the lamp and follows me to my old bedroom so that I don't stumble on the dusty runner rug or a loose floorboard. Then she takes the stairs to the creaky loft and is halfway up before turning. "Goodnight Darcy. Sleep sweet."

"Night, Mama." I yawn wide and it forces my eyes shut. When I open them again, I'm engulfed in the dark.

My bed is the same. The sheets are the same: itchy and pink with lace trimmings tucked tight into the whitewashed wire frame. I've always liked the look of a daybed. There's something romantic and sophisticated about them. Except this one is rusted and the back has an enormous heart curled into the design, so all I can think about is blood pulsing. And then not pulsing. In a fit of sympathy, Aunt Lou purchased an identical bed to help me transition when I first moved in with her. It didn't last long, however, before Aunt Lou decided I was old enough for something more practical. She traded the daybed for a full-size mattress and box, with a pale wooden frame devoid of any romantic embellishments. The daybed I'd come to love so much and seek comfort in, the way most people find the smell of freshly baked sugar cookies, laid in a pile of metal rods on the kerb for a week until the trash collectors came. I cried when the men bundled up the skeleton and tossed it into the back of the truck. Aunt Lou said, and I know she only meant it as a comfort and not a betrayal, "When I was I child I spoke as I child. I played as a child. But now it is time to put away childish things."

I tried to hate her for getting rid of the daybed without asking me first, but she smoothed down my hair when she spoke. My parents never held me tight for anything, not even when I split my knees open on the rocks by the creek. So I understood, even if I didn't have the words for it, that Aunt Lou was helping me. Or, at least, trying to be good.

I sit on the edge of the original daybed and give it a few experimental bounces before removing my shoes and socks. Then I have to fumble in the dark for my pajamas. The house continues to pulse in the autumn wind. Pulse and then not pulse, like it swallowed the rhythm in Daddy's chest.

It's unholy dark but I'm not tired. There's enough coloured paper on the windows of my bedroom door that I'm sure, if I put it to night mode, Mama wouldn't even notice the shine of my cellphone. I yank back the itchy pink and white afghan blanket and the overstretched pink sheets underneath.

The lace border of the small pillow tickles my neck and the bed rocks with each movement, squeaking boldly. It makes me think of historical movie sex and I stop wriggling around. If the light of my phone doesn't get Mama's attention, then the sound will. I don't want her mad at me. I have to be good. I slowly inhale the smell of grease and mothballs. I have to stay quiet.

All I wanted to do was scroll through my friends' pages, see how they spent their first day at the beach, but the service keeps dropping and I can't connect to the internet. I press the phone against me, feeling the warmth of the battery on my sternum. Not tired. Had I always had trouble sleeping in this house?

Maybe it's because I was thinking of sex or because the silence unnerved me in ways I never expected, but I reach over to my purse hanging off the bed knob beside my head and fish out the business card Gagandeep gave me. The paper is thick enough I could clean my nails with one of the corners if

I wanted. The embossed lettering is smooth and cool beneath my thumb. I didn't see a landline next to the cash register and I start to wonder if this is a cell number. I type it slowly into my phone, one eye closed, using the light of the screen to read the card.

Hey you.

A tiny blue-green circle appears next to my speech bubble. Sending. Sending. It probably is for a landline or I'm too far in the hills for any message to go through. Minutes pass and I think about Daddy sitting out there on the edge of the woods next to his homemade burner. My heart sticks in my throat and the back of my teeth hurt from clenching down.

A memory I can't scrape at pulls me, tugs me, like I'm waiting for a turn on a theme park ride I know will kill me but I refuse to step out of line. The closer I get to the memory, the more my pulse quickens. The house creaks and thumbs in the wind, louder and louder, itching at me, trying to expose the memory.

*

"Daddy. Why can't I help make charcoal?"

"The charcoal burner has tales to tell. He lives in the forest, alone in the forest; he sits in the forest, alone in the forest. And the sun comes slanting between the trees."

The grass is damp against my feet. Was damp. Is damp. I'm scared and small and Mama told me to hide and the house isn't big enough to hide in. I'll be found. I must not be found. I slip out the window. My nightgown snags and I run to the trees. The forest is full of shadows, wild boars, coyotes, rings of mushrooms that can snatch me. The charcoal mound is huge and I can hide there. Behind it? Inside it. Moss and hay sponges around my hands. The moon is full and white like teeth, and there is ash and strips of wood, white like teeth, in the bottom of the pit.

*

My phone buzzes in my palm and I open my eyes with a shuddering breath. I wasn't sure what I had seen in the charcoal burner and the pale impression of a child's scream touches my throat. I was still there at sunrise, watching the mist come off the grass waiting for someone to save me. Whatever I saw that night, I know it has something to do with how my memory has been wiped into one dirty smudge. That poem...I had thought it was just something Daddy liked to say whenever I asked him why I couldn't help him and why I couldn't come near the mound while he worked. I never heard it again until my poetry class, when we finished with Yeats and moved on to Milne.

He lives in the forest. Alone in the forest.

Again my phone buzzes and I finally unlock the screen to read two messages. Both are from Gagandeep.

Ouch. I thought we were friends.

It's late. You okay?

So I answer.

Yes. I can't sleep.

It takes a few minutes for it to send. Then he responds.

And you're thinking of me? ;p

I grin and I'm glad he doesn't know this because I want to stay cool and collected. If he's the knight in shining armour and I'm the seductress, I have to play the part. Besides, a little light flirting never hurt anyone. In fact, it was so perfectly normal that my breathing settled and the itching buzz in my veins slowly made its way out of my system.

Why should I let anyone sleep when I can't?

The amount of time it takes for our messages to go through is like some kind of cerebral foreplay. Did I say the right thing? How will he respond? I hope he smiles. I hope I smile. I hope we forget all about this by morning.

Why can't you sleep? he asks.

The woods are haunted, I tell him.

You are very brave to live so close. he says.

Only because I know you're near. I say.

Want me to come and slay the dragon?

What if I am the dragon?

Want me to come and slay you?

You're welcome to try. I can add your sword to those who fought and died valiantly before you.

I smile, thinking how clever I am. Then I remember that in poetry you're supposed to read between the lines and I've made myself sound like I sleep around. Except, if I sent another text to clarify I didn't mean sword as in penis, it would ruin the momentum. But I don't want Gagandeep thinking I'm the type that has a new partner every weekend. I'm starting to think I've made a real mess of it by putting on the pressure too quick, especially when I didn't mean it, but another text comes in and I breathe a little sigh of relief. I'm not sure if it's Mama's attempt at pancakes poisoning me but the walls are closer. The pink wallpaper warps and tears, leaning over me, as the wooden boards beneath it pull away from the frame to close down on me like the lid of a coffin.

My cellphone buzzes and I blink. The walls are back where

they should be. My stomach gurgles and the indigestion reaches my head, poking at the skin above my eyebrows. It's got to be food poisoning. An allergic reaction to all that lard.

My armor is in the shop until morning. (Baba has me working the night shift. Like anyone stops here.) I will bring plastic wrapped pastries to the all-powerful dragon if she finds this tribute suitable?

Just like that, we're on even footing again.

Bear claws?

Only the best.

...I'll allow it.

Be prepared for battle at sunrise! Seriously, be prepared. These things are a bitch to open!

I tell him goodnight and lay my phone face down beside my pillow. It feels good to be silly with someone and forget about the unnerving way the house breathes and scratches at me. Now, with a smile burning my cheeks, sleep comes easy.

Chapter Five

My first week at college, already weighed down with homesickness and uncertain that I'd be able to hack dorm life, I signed up as a test subject in the psychology department. At best, I'd meet a few people that could hopefully become long-term friends. At worst, I'd have one hundred dollars in my pocket. As it turned out, the test was more of an extended lecture on the benefits of hypnosis. Before the magician (or was it mentalist?) started in on the practical examples, he went on a long tangent about the Greeks and how they believed the soul travelled when we dreamed. Something like that. I sort of tuned in and out, not wanting to lock eyes with anyone in case I was made to stand on the chair and yodel. Later I learned that hypnosis only worked if I was willing and I couldn't be made to do something against my base nature. "Like murder!" the magician laughed. The other students laughed. I didn't. I wasn't sure. Could the desire to hack someone apart be genetic, dormant in me until I'm triggered?

Although I hadn't paid close enough attention to learn how a wandering soul and hypnosis, some vague notion of the extraordinary and limitless powers of the mind, "What if dreams are a parallel universe and when we sleep, or are put to sleep, those are the only times we can access the other side?" swirled in my thoughts as I looked down at my bedroom.

I know this is a dream because I know I am myself. I feel my own skin and bones and dark hair brushing against my forehead, even though I can't see evidence of my body. I know it must be a dream because I'm staring at my younger self. I must have been around eight years old. Thin, dark hair pulled into two tiny braids flop down pointy shoulders. The naked bulb shines into all the corners of the room. Pink and yellow everywhere. On the wall, on the bed, on the flannel nightgown.

Daddy sits at the edge of the bed. He's dressed down to his undershirt and jeans. Feet bare. I forgot how big his arms were, how round his face was. I reach out for him, knowing my hand is stretching to touch his back, still damp from hard labor, but I don't see my body and I begin to drift, phantom that I am.

He tucks little me into the bed, pushing the blanket so that I'm trapped to the mattress. I giggle. Me, as I am, little me, as I was.

"Will you tell me something?" It's the child-self that asks, but I feel my mouth curve around the words each time she speaks. So I know that this dream is also a memory and I try to taste the words that come out of my mouth, the way Daddy always did when he spoke.

"What sort of something?"

"A story. Make it a good one."

"Hmm. A good one. An important one." He drums his thick, callused fingers against his hard chin, which is dusted with peppery stubble. "Once upon a time," he starts this way because all the good stories begin with a 'once', with a distance between the teller and the listener, because it means it's a warning. If it was a 'once', then it will happen a 'twice', and he wants me to understand. I remember how he told Mama all the time, "Darcy is small but that doesn't mean she can't be prepared."

"Once upon a time, there was a young man who could find no work in his small village. His mother and sisters were hungry and the law men were coming to take the king's monthly taxes. So of course the young man needed to make enough money to pay the king and to have stuff to buy for winter."

"What kinda stuff?" I shift my head, squinting because the light bulb hurts my tender eyes.

"Cheese with blue veins and brown bread and dried, twisted meat that wouldn't get spoiled."

"How come his mama didn't go? How come his sisters don't help?" I wriggle my hand out from the blanket and grab his large fingers, pulling them apart and pushing them at the knuckles. He lets me explore the shape of his hands.

"Because a long time ago, people thought women had to stay home and it was very silly. But that meant the boy had to travel to the next town to look for work. Only he had never been before. He had never been outside of his village and he was scared to go alone in the wood, but his mama said he would be okay as long as he stayed on the path. She told him to bring a knife and it would take a whole day to walk. 'Keep to the path' she kept saying. 'Don't talk to strangers and keep to the path.'"

"Did he?"

"He tried. But that night, the cold came in and he had to stop and make shelter. So he went to cut down branches to build a hutch and a fire."

"Is he Red Riding Hood?"

A big chuckle escapes him and he shakes his head. "You'd think! But no, she wasn't the only one who didn't listen to the rules of the forest."

I nod. Daddy always tells me those rules and the first is always stick to the path so I don't get lost. He clears his throat. "So he goes looking for a place to camp, except it was dark and the trees were very big and thick with leaves. There was no moonlight to help guide him. He began to cry and shiver and cry. He was lost and alone. It started to snow and he knew that he would die."

I whisper, "Did he die?"

"No," Daddy hesitates on the word like he wants to say something else but changes his mind. "He whistled into the dark. He called out for help. 'Please! Is there anyone who can help me? Please! I'm so cold! If you help me I'll give you anything you want!' but no one heard him. So he kept walking. *Crunch-crunch-crunch* through the bramble and the snow that came in thick. Eventually he found the path again. He knew it was the path because the trees became thinner and the moon came through. He kept walking because he was so cold. Then it became hard to breathe and hard to see."

"Did he make a fire?"

"There was too much snow for it," Daddy says with a sad tone and then he adds a breathy, "but suddenly!" and I squeak. He smiles and closes his fingers around mine. "A woman appeared before him! She was tall and elegant. Her hair carried the glow of one thousand stars and her face was pointed and beautiful like a fox. She said 'Young man. Do you need help?' and he said, 'Yes! Please! I'm so cold,' and she said, 'I will give you my coat so you can stay warm tonight but tomorrow you must give me a coat so that I will not be cold.' The young man trembled at the power of her voice. 'Yes, I promise.' and she gave him her coat. It was made of soft, thick fur, red as fire! The snow around him melted and the tall woman vanished. The young man made a clearing in the snow for himself and fell asleep under the oven warmth of his new coat.

"The next morning, he arrived at the village and traded the goods his mother asked him to sell. Then, with money and supplies in his pocket, he took the path back home. Again he stopped to sleep along the path. It was very dark and very cold, colder than the night before, but he was glad for his coat. He was asleep for many hours before the woman appeared. The shimmering glow off her hair woke the young man. 'It's still very cold,' he told her. 'Will you walk with me tonight and I will give you the coat in the morning?' She considered his request, then smiled wide and he saw all her teeth and when she said, 'I will walk with you tonight and you will give me two coats in the morning'. He was frightened because he didn't understand what she meant, but he knew that he'd made a mistake with her. Then she vanished again. The young man didn't know where she was but knew he had to stand up and continue his walk home."

I know this is a dream because while Daddy tells the story, figures glide from the nearby trees and fold into the bedroom. A young man. An impossibly beautiful woman. Her teeth are the edge of a saw and the young man removes the fur coat, bowing to her, calves trembling, neck exposed.

"It was dawn when he approached the mouth of the trail that led him to his village. Once again, the woman appeared. 'Now you will give me two coats,' she said. She took the one he borrowed from her and then she took his skin from his bones and slipped into it, wrapping herself tightly. 'Ah,' she said, 'This is a very good coat.'"

Chapter Six

The muscles in my arms and jaw are clenched so tight I'm ripped awake. I gag into the pillow. unable to shake off the image of the young man flayed by unseen forces. One moment he bowed and the next, the ropes of muscle and tendon were exposed to the naked bulb while his skin fell like a silk shift to the floorboards.

My arms and legs crumple toward my centre until I'm nothing more than a dying spider, waiting to be swept into the cracks. I breathe through my teeth until my heart slows, and I can hear the moan of the house again. The dream keeps scratching, in the same way that the memories are scratching, just below the surface. Unreachable and prickly. *Look at us. Notice us. Listen. Do you understand?*

I stretch out, testing my joints with each roll and pop. My toenail snags on the pilling blanket. What I need is fresh air. What I need is to not be in this house for a few minutes. Coming here was a mistake. There's an analogue alarm clock by the window with its little hands moving toward the two o'clock hour. Its soda-green face is the only light and it guides me as I shuffle across the room, failing to avoid the stacked boxes. *Tick. Tick. Tick. Tick. Tick.*

Everything sounds so loud now: the swish of my skin against the faded turquoise carpet, the gentle sway of my nightdress, the drag of the curtains. Metal on metal. A knife unsheathed. The window snags when I push on it. It's been painted shut, but the paint peels easily beneath my fingernail, like dead skin shedding off a sunburn. The hinge groans and spits, but eventually the air comes in with the smell of wet grass and horse manure.

It's only then that I realise there's nothing: no crickets and bullfrogs. No rustling of leaves. Or owl hooting. Or wild boar rutting. Even the house has stopped settling into its joists. It's dead and still. If it weren't for the moon, I might have thought a tornado was about to touch down. Out across the yard, toward the bramble and the thickets beyond Daddy's charcoal pit, the shadows warp and shimmer, the way heat comes off the tarmac, trying to convince you there's water in the dips of the road. It might be more fog catching in the deeper parts where the moonlight can't reach. What else could it be? There is nothing shifting the dead leaves. There is nothing alive in the forest.

The strange silence numbs me, draws me into it, until I feel like I'm standing on the edge of the yard. I am. I'm here in the grass, toes curling into the soft black dirt. The charcoal pit vibrates and hums into my bones like an omen, like I'm meant to crawl inside the way I had done as a child. I don't even remember climbing out of the window but its old mouth stares at me. It has a mind of its own, like the house. It sits in the forest. Alone in the forest.

Along the rim, where the chimney collapsed, twigs and straw sway. Only there is no wind to tease the old bits of the structure upward and out. Yet there it is, thin little needles with joints running down the incredible length. Twigs moving the way fingers move when snatching for a coin stuck in the back of a drawer. More twigs shift and tap along the broken edge. They slide down, looking more like squared-off hand bones with each passing second, and they are passing. *Tick. Tick. Tick. Tick.*

I'm not sure how long I've been standing at the open window, mesmerised by the haunting quiet, but I can't pull away. I know if I turn my eyes to look at the time, I'll miss something important. I'm stuck in the headlights of unknowing. So I keep watching the twigs shimmy and wriggle. Like fingers. Like worms. Pulsing and tapping on the top of the mound that rises and falls with the same uneven rhythm of a deflated lung.

A figure moves to the left of the mound, bone white and shifting between the staggered post oaks. I turn to see what it is and feel the snap of fishing wire break free from my brain. When I look back at the mound, there's nothing there. The straw and twigs aren't disturbed. I know what I saw but I'm not so sure as I was a few seconds ago. Or was it minutes? I'm back inside, standing at the window. My hand runs down the soft wood and the cold air crackles in my lungs. My gaze flickers to the clock balanced on a narrow box. It's three o'clock in the morning. I've been standing by the window for an hour. My skin is raised and damp from the gust of wind that sweeps in. Browning leaves chatter as they push and shove for their spot in the branches over the roof. Movement in the forest again. It's so loud, so full of chirping, yelping, croaking, hooting, that it overwhelms me. I slam the window shut and reflected in the glass are fangs and matted fur. An unhinged jaw. Cracked eye sockets with maggots dribbling down sunken cheeks. It's transplanted over the silhouette of my face and I'm shrieking, unable to stop. I keep at it until my throat is raw and Mama thunders down the stairs and bursts into the room. She grabs me by the shoulder and slaps me across the face. I stumble back from her, cradling the sting in my cheek. She pulls the curtains with a furious yank. She hisses, "What were you thinking?"

A rush of fabric and boxes tumble over as she drags me into the heart of the house. My knees sting from where they've been jabbed by the corners of falling boxes. Mama ignores my pleas for her to stop or, at least, slow down. She grips my fingers so tight that the knuckles pop and fold together. I know I'm going to die. She doesn't even need a good reason. There is no good reason. I had a nightmare. I opened the curtains. Mama likes the silence and I screamed. And now I'm dead. My eyes sweep the darkness for the silhouette of an axe. I don't see one anywhere, but that doesn't mean it's not tucked away within arm's reach.

She slings me on the couch and the armrest knocks against my ribs, stealing my breath. "You know better! We raised you better than this!" She snaps, her voice a low roll of thunder. The darkness is so heavy. Her voice travels. I'm not sure where she is in the room. "What did I tell you about calling things into the house?"

I stutter, unable to get the words out fast enough. "L-light brings the m-monsters in....We s-stay quiet so they don't know w-we're here."

"All it takes is one whistle, one shout into the dark, to put us in danger!" Her voice is deeper in the house. Or is it beside me, but so quiet I only think she's far away?

When I was in the fifth grade, the class went on a field trip to Cascade Caverns and the tour guide turned off the lights to show us how the blackness engulfed everything. She wanted us to know what it would feel like to be lost in the cave. I couldn't breathe then and I can't breathe now. I can't see. I feel weightless and powerless to the frantic shuffling coming from Mama. There's no telling where she is, flapping around like a bat, clutching for something to grab onto, to snare. To bite.

Oh, God. She's looking for an axe!

Before I can catch my breath and worm my way out of the room, the familiar hiss of gas and a struck match comes seconds before Mama's face is illuminated by the lamp. Her eyes are hollows in the paper-thin folds of skin. Her wrinkled lips pull back and the yellow of her teeth shine with the saliva that's gathered in the pockets of her cheeks. "What did you do?"

I shake my head and Mama digs her nails into my shoulder. Her barely-there eyebrows bunch together and her eyes shine wide, like she's panicked. But the way she speaks is the way she always angrily grounds out cigarette butts. "Don't make me ask again."

This is the woman Aunt Lou warned me about. I shake my head again. "I had a bad dream. I just wanted fresh air."

"You *don't* get just fresh air!" She shrieks in that harsh, breathy way when she struggles to keep quiet. "Not at night! You know better!"

She turns away, ashamed of me. "Did you even bother to listen to the things your father taught you?"

With that question, she puts holes in my bones. I stare at my socked feet. I can't look at her. Is she's going to kill me because I've disappointed her or because I was loud? Maybe when she goes to get the axe, I can escape through the living room window. Sure, I'd have to live with the shame for the rest of my life. But that's just it. I'll be alive.

Except she stands at the window, muttering into the curtains as she draws a pattern in the air with a stubby finger. She spits on the floor and then moves to the next window. She repeats the muttering and pattern drawing. She spits again.

"Stay there." Mama takes the lamp and moves silently out of the room, leaving me to be swallowed whole by the dark.

Chapter Seven

What am I supposed to do when my mother tells me to stay put? I'm terrified that she's going to kill me, that she lured me here to help her pack only because she wants to finish what she started with Daddy. I don't know why she would. Aunt Lou never said exactly Mama's reason, and the investigation never exactly proved Mama held the axe or that the murder was premeditated. These last seven years, I'd clung to this idea that everything was a huge misunderstanding. Mama is innocent! Mama is a victim of the system! The last ten minutes have started to severely sway my opinion.

Last time Mama told me to stay put, I jumped out of my bedroom window. Then Daddy died and Mama was stuck here in this tiny house on the hill, by the edge of the forest. Alone in the forest.

This time I listen. I wait. The echo of her quick footsteps are the pulse of the house and the wind pushing against the old wood, making the shudders clack against the frame, is the rickety breath of whatever is outside. A rhythmic tapping against the window plucks at the strings of fear that are tied at my throat. Still, I turn my head towards it, as though I could see through the piercing dark and beyond the heavy curtains.

"Is it raining?" Asking feels like a normal thing to do. Unobtrusive. Small. Mama doesn't hear me. She doesn't answer. Her quick little feet are in the kitchen now. As quietly as I can, I push myself off the couch. My thumb briefly falls into a small, burnt circle where a Virginia Slim left its mark and the floorboards squeak. I wait. When she doesn't come to shove me into place, I move from the couch to the wall, the paper almost like velvet against my cheek and peek into the kitchen to see what she's doing. She drags cans and glass jars from the mouldy pantry, muttering. The wind blows and creaks. It's either acorns pattering down the roof and window or it's actually started raining. Curious, I slide toward the window, keeping my feet on the rug to dampen the noise. Mama says stay but I'm not leaving the room. I just want to look out and watch the rain muddy the yard. That's all. I want to prove to myself that it's ordinary nature, not one of Daddy's hodags from the stories come to play a tormenting game with me.

There's nothing outside to be worried about. Of course there isn't. The itch and dig of old memories is lying. It's only the inside of the house that troubles me. Mama. She's unstable. She's lost herself and I don't want to be on the wrong side of her. I never should have snooped into Aunt Lou's things. If I minded my own business, I wouldn't have found the stacks of letters from Mama, showing that she wanted me. Showing that she never left this house and waited for my return. Did I do something at dinner that changed her mind? Did she realise that I wasn't the child she wanted but a grown woman and a stranger?

Minutes pass. Hours? I haven't done more than hover between the couch and curtains but my eyes are adjusting.

It helps that the pool of lamplight has wormed its way into the living room, fanning out from the swinging door that separates me from the kitchen. Mama's making something. Stirring. Smashing. Muttering.

It isn't anything at all to open the curtains. It's easy. She wouldn't know. Stay in this room. She didn't necessarily mean stay seated. Did she? Besides, she might have an axe after all and I have escaped out the window before. From here, it wouldn't be more than a jump to my...oh. I need my car keys first.

I curl a nail around the green and ivy curtains. A flutter of menthol burns my nostrils, forcing me into uneven breaths. The fabric is thick and scratchy. The tapping stops the moment I've got a slit apart in the fabric. Acorns then. Has to be. How dark is it outside? It feels like someone is staring me down through the fabric, waiting for me to flick open the curtains wide.

"What are you doing?" Mama gasps. She rushes to grip my fingers and drag me away from the window. My knuckles pop and snap but she doesn't let go and the flickering kerosene light between us turns her waxy. The deep-set eyes and tight mouth turn her into a horrible creature made of chalk and drawn into the road, smudged with rain.

"I wanted to see if it was raining."

"You've seen rain before!" she snaps. "Stay away from the windows. It knows you're in the house with all that noise you make. That doesn't mean we have to spotlight your every movement!"

"Why?"

"Why what?" She looks down with searing disbelief. I'm three again and in trouble because I kicked the shins of Miss

Loretta during Sunday School when I should have been colouring the lions in the den with Danial. God, I hated those picture books. The covers were always detailed and beautiful but the insides were blown-out features, roly-poly blobs in cloth only vaguely resembling a human. Why wouldn't a little kid be upset about that? Of course I thought Miss Lotty had tricked me and wouldn't give me the good pictures to colour. Mama didn't say anything. She stares me down. Daddy drove us home so she could keep staring me down until we were back inside the house and she dragged me by the knuckles to my bedroom, where I stayed the rest of the day. No meals to distract me from thinking about what I'd done.

"What knows I'm here?"

Mama clicks her tongue and her eyes roll. Slick, glossy whites in the black caves made by the lamplight. "Don't be an idiot. Or does nothing stay in that head?"

She's never acted this way towards me. It's as if I'm meeting her for the first time. Abrasive. Cold. Expectations too big for a heart too small.

"I'm not trying to be." The words get stuck behind my teeth. "I don't know–"

"Yes," she snaps. "You do. I just can't think of why...it's not like you went outside and whistled for something to come follow you?" Her dark eyes narrow until I can't see more than a thin film of her pupils. "Did you?"

The lamp slides onto the coffee table and she fills her hands with a box of Virginia Slims and book of matches. She lights one and inhales deeply, shaking the match out. I curl my body in, knees and shoulders kissing each other, wanting to disappear. I don't tell her I had the window down while I listened to the radio.

When she chooses to sit in the floral print armchair instead of beside me on the sofa, a tiny bit of relief works its way into my veins. The further she is away from me, the safer I feel. I never should have come.

Mama's lips pucker around the cigarette and she pats the side of her head, checking the stiffness of those painted red curls. "You know."

Acorns scatter down the roof and across the windows. *Tatattatt. Tatattatt.* Nails against the glass. The slicks of Mama's eyes roam over to the window, irritated, as though an unwanted guest is trying to get her attention and she's waiting for him to take the hint and go away.

"You've forgotten the woods." Her quiet tone rattles me out of the stupor I had sunk into. "You didn't keep the lessons of your father."

"How could I?" My hands are cold and I press them against my neck, warm and flushed. "He's dead."

"So? Because he dies everything has to go with him? Do you burn the memories the way you would a photograph?" Mama shakes her head and the *tatattatt* shifts from the window to the space between the walls.

"Sounds like a squirrel–"

"Ha!" Mama tilts ashes into an open Altoid tin. She hasn't spoken above a whisper. That alone is frightening enough but then she says. "Go on outside if you think it's only a squirrel and some rain." When I don't move, she squints through the curling ribbons of smoke. "Go on. Get."

The curve of Mama's chin juts upward, pulling the leathery skin tight, erasing the thin avenues of wrinkles that have slowly erased her former beauty. Smoke slips between the crack in her mouth, floats upward, and she smiles. Unhappy, mocking, satisfied in my inability to stand. I want to prove to her that I'm not afraid, and I know she's tricking me into submission, but my legs are hot glue and syrup. Animal enthusiasts always warn about turning your back on big cats because, the moment you do, that's when they sneak up behind you, sink their teeth into your neck and claw your face off. Mama's red, press-on nails might not be sharp enough to do the dirty work, but I've never forgotten that she has an axe and Daddy's body was never found.

My joints are all stiff but the rest of me wobbles and shakes in the attempt to detach myself from the sofa. I know without asking that Mama won't let me take the kerosene lamp. I take a steadying breath, lungs full and crackling with secondhand menthol. I'd forgotten how long it took to shake the smell of cigarettes out of all my clothes. I miss the rosy undercurrent and the crisp bright minimal design of Aunt Lou's house. I never should have come here. The walk out of the room and down the hall feels like a trap. What I've got to do is wait until she's asleep, then sneak out to the car and shift it into neutral, slide down the hill never to return. I'll block her number. I'll change my name. A nice clean cut... I'll tell Aunt Lou I'm sorry.

A bubble of plaster presses against my palm as I use the wall to guide me to the front door. The fan of light coming from the lamp's small flame diminishes enough for me to know that she's turning down the gas. She doesn't want the light to chase after me when I open the door. The hinges creak and her whisper, barely louder than my footsteps were, follows me. "Don't step off the porch." Her breath is wet and smoky on my neck. I turn with a gasp, hand pressed against the exposed skin, but Mama isn't there.

Mist rolls off the grass and the sky is empty. A cold flush of moonlight nearly blinds me. It was so dark inside this feels like an LED flashing across my face, like when my friends and I were pulled over after a night of drinking.

License and Registration. Do you know how fast you're going?

Not fast at all. I'm sitting right here.

There's no wind in the trees, not a single hint of acorns falling onto the roof. The trees closest to the house aren't even oak, they're hackberries. Further out are the cedar and post oaks. Their low branches spread out and dip in arthritic curves, obscuring the shadows that dart through them. Voles. Owls. My teeth chatter and the damp clings to me, sneaking up my nightgown. The axe is no longer by my muddy shoes. There's not a sound in the world, except for my uneven breath and the cigarette paper curling close to Mama's lips. I turn again, but it's only me on the porch. There's markings scratched into the woods of the pillars that I never noticed before. Zigzag shapes that remind me of crop circles.

When everything in front of you is hidden and only the moonlight guides you, shapes turn into tricks. The horizon isn't rich and layered with trees, undergrowth, rock and grass. It all flattens out and presses down like the cardboard backing of a diorama. The wind is low but unmoving. How? The hackberry trees are stiff and silent but the howling is distinctly the rustle of leaves. It's only a whisper. *Heey. Heey. Darcy. Daaarcyyy. Where aaarrrreee yooooouuuu?*

"I'm here," I whisper back. I think I whisper. The cold bites at my toes and I curl my arms around me, like the unseen wind is cutting into me.

Then. There it is. I see it.

Out of the matte black of the horizon, something moves. Stained ivory clicks against bark, moves around the curve of a tree. The yellow-orange swirl of an eye catching the moon. It looks at me. It sees me, deep down, like its gaze is trying to pull me from my throat and out my own eyes.

A hand latches onto my shoulder and then presses over my mouth before I can scream. Claws dig into fabric, skin and bone. I'm yanked inside and the door slams shut. I stumble over my loose socks and fall to the ground, nearly clipping the sharp corner of the bottom step. My voice catches, buried back into my throat.

"You saw it."

I shake my head. Then nod.

"Good. Go sit down and we will discuss. Hopefully you remember now."

Dust and the uneven grain of the floorboards dig into my skin. My arms can't support me but my legs refuse to uncurl. Mama takes me by the elbow and helps me up. Then she pulls a long, thin boning knife from the pocket of her quilted housecoat. The elkhorn handle is stark against her dark shape, almost like it's her own bone breaking through the skin. My muscles spasm. If this is going to be the last thing I see before she kills me, I'm glad I'm standing.

Mama turns away from me and she kneels in front of the door and carves a strange symbol into the softened wood. The scraping and swishing shine of the blade moves with expertise. Its buttery hiss cuts through the sounds outside. Whatever it is, this thing, it shrieks like newborn rabbits.

"Michael will protect us," she says. "Go back to the living room and sit."

Chapter Eight

The Vicks-scented tissue is in pieces in my lap and my fingers are covered in oil that's meant to soothe my nose. At least it smells better than the smoke. I'm beyond crying. I haven't been able to, even though the well in me is so close to bursting my eyes are bouncing in the waves and the skin around my nose and forehead pulls tight. For the first time, I realise how strange it is to not have a back door to the house.

The lower half of the house consists only of the living room, kitchen and my bedroom. Mama and Daddy slept in the loft at the top of the stairs. My bedroom is beside the stairs. The front door is beside my bedroom. Mama is at the front door. In the living room, beyond the curtain is the *tattattat* that roots me to the dim glow of the kerosene lamp. The thought of sprinting into the kitchen and using the narrow window above the sink crosses my mind. Before I can will myself into action, Mama comes back into the room and eases me onto the sofa. She gently tugs the box of tissues out of my trembling hands. "What use are they if you tear them up?"

She slides the box of Virginia Slims closer to her. The cardboard grates against the wood. She taps a cigarette against the curve of her palm and her long nails clack together when she brings the cigarette to her lips and strikes a match. The lick of flame ignites her wide, deep-set eyes. It makes me think of the creature outside with its overlarge features glowing against the blue moon.

"I told you to stay on the porch," she says.

"I did!"

"Then why are your feet covered in grass?"

She's not wrong. When I lift up my nightgown, I'm startled to see clippings of green-yellow blades stuck to my ankles and the toe end of my socks. A little blood and skin is torn on my heel. "I think I walked out my window. When I was dreaming."

"I see."

"Will it come in?" I ask on a trembling inhale.

"It stays at the window." Mama rubs her temple; the lit cigarette briefly disappears into her set curls before she brings it down to her mouth again. "It stays at the door...but the way you've carried on? Who knows. It could have found a way in."

"But what is it?" My mouth is gummy but I don't touch the warm Dr. Slice she put in front of me.

She shifts. Fat toes poke out from underneath the housecoat. The nails are painted the same red as her press-ons, but it only highlights the hard, cracked skin of her feet instead of distracting from it. "It has lots of names. I won't speak them. Each culture gives it a name and each name holds such power that it's as good as an invitation. Any one of them could give it enough power to break the wards I've spent years perfecting to protect this home." Mama shakes her hair. Old, thin skin wobbles, like it's loose on her skull. Smoke swirls blue-grey. Her hair remains unmoving.

"But *what* is it?" I ask, more desperate this time. Maybe

if I understand, then I can figure out a way to get out before Mama's craziness turns physical. I don't want to become just another stain on the wall.

She takes her time, inhaling the dry menthol-laced tobacco into her lungs and pushes it back out her nose. Our shadows dance across the ceiling, and the blue-white flame of the kerosene lamp hisses low on the wick. Just a few hours to dawn. Then what? Can I make my escape then? Will the sun push out the wild frenzy in Mama's eyes?

"Sometimes their names mean 'not of one skin'. You remember. You must. Your daddy used to say 'he goes on all fours.'"

The backs of my knees ache. My fingers curl against the armrest because my heart is in my throat and I feel like I'm drowning. She speaks about him so calmly; I suspect she's fishing for a reaction. Although I can't know her motives to do this, I know it's best to stay calm when cornered with an irrational person. To keep myself passive, I dig the curve of my thumb into the cigarette burn and pluck at the thin strands of fabric.

"I don't remember," I managed to whisper. Outside, the tapping stops and is replaced with the shriek of baby rabbits. Daddy once told a story about The Good Neighbors hiding beneath a window and mimicking sounds of a crying human so that they might trick a sympathetic person to come outside and ensnare them. Rabbits sound so much like babies, it's almost unbearable. Mama sighs and I quickly stop plucking at the armrest. I fold my hands together, balancing them in the cotton hammock my nightgown makes between my knees.

"I just don't understand why it's back. It's stayed in the woods for years." She speaks to herself, smashing the unsmoked half of her cigarette into the Altoid tin. "I seen it on the road but it runs off. What now? You?"

Her gaze snaps to me and I freeze. Me? Does the confession of the song on my radio blast across my face the way it shot through the dark before I lost signal? Could something so simple be the reason for our sudden troubles? "I-I. I didn't do anything."

She shakes her head. "You opened the window."

"I had a bad dream."

"You screamed."

"It was a dream!"

Mama doesn't move from her chair and I want the floor to swallow me whole. The way she looks at me, worse than all the other times, gets the small hairs on my knuckles to rise. She stands, rocks back and forth. There's a moment of hesitation, like she's going to walk over to the bookshelf and get something but it's all been packed. Only a few lonely figurines remain in their dusty spots.

"Whistles in the dark," she says as a small apathetic grin stretches her loose mouth thin. I'm not sure what to say or if I'm allowed to speak. What if making excuses only nails the lid to my coffin? The hard angle of her shoulders slump. "I've packed all the books."

"We can look for them?" I suggest. Already the cold dread that consumed me is leaking out. This all had to be a trick of some kind, a scare tactic because I've upset her. I didn't eat dinner like I was supposed to. Or…Or I used my phone and the light was bright. Was it because I turned on the taps and Mama said the pipes made it too loud? She's just tricking me to teach me a lesson. After all, I did tell her I had a nightmare and that's what started all this. She must be playing on the fear and adrenaline that's kept me so confused. I have to learn this lesson quick because she has the hunting glint in her eyes. It's the same as it was seven years ago. The startling clarity of her gaze turns my spine into ice, ready to shatter upon impact.

To give myself something to do, I pick up the Dr. Slice and pop it open. The liquid bubbles and hisses out like an angry rattlesnake. I drop the can and it spins under the coffee table. Mama's head turns in my direction and I shrink down, grabbing tissue to clean the mess before it sets into the rug. Most of it is absorbed in my nightgown.

"This is Church business," she begins, turning back to the empty shelves, using the indentations of dust to spark her own memories on the subject. "Capital 'c' Church." Mama inhales, hands on her hips, and coughs. She considers the package of Virginia Slims, shakes it to only find two inside and sets it down again. In all this time, the pale screaming outside hasn't stopped, like it's getting all the energy out of one swelling lung that doesn't need to pause to refill with air. Mama stares at the heavy velvet curtains. "Not the sort of thing they teach you down at the local First Baptist. This is old knowledge, and people don't read enough to know nothing about it."

Mama walks over and I lean back. It's now. It's happening. She's talking about religion and that's what always happens in those news stories of mothers who kill their children. Do her fingers feel like paper? Are they cold? Instead of wrapping them around my neck, she takes the sopping tissues and empty can of Dr. Slice. With surprising strength, she crumples the can in one hand, then stuffs everything into the now empty tissue box.

The relief is palpable and she notices I've flinched from her. I wiggle back into my seat on the sofa and sit on my hands.

I feel like I should pray for my survival but I haven't done that in years. What would I say anyway? *Please, God. You don't know me, but I'd really like it if I didn't die tonight.*

"Now. Church business. To begin with…No. That won't do. I need to think. The devil with that thing out there! It's too loud!" Mama slams her tiny feet against the floor and a little cloud of dust catches in the glow of the lamp. The oil is running out and I can only hope that means it'll be daybreak soon and all this awfulness can be put behind me.

"There's an old story. I think that's best. If you know the root of it. Your daddy tried to tell it to you in bedtime stories but *clearly* it never took. You always played too close to the woods and his charcoal burner."

"But what—"

"That's enough interruptions!" She slices the nicotine sticky air with her hand and then clamps her jaw shut, taking a steadying inhale through her narrow nose. "This old story, see? It was back when Jesus was just a spit of an idea and priests were popping up all over the damn place, like you wouldn't believe! Anyway. There's this one. Some say Saint Patrick. Yes, the same one. The documents from Giraldus Cambrensis are all sealed and I've only heard the account from your daddy, see? He had it in a book, but I've put that away ages ago. Might be up in the attic." Mama shakes her head and wiggles free a Virginia Slim. She lights it. "So this Saint So-n-so was sent off to Ireland. At the time known as the Island of Wolves to the Britons and the Romans and blah-de-blah. Old magic likes to put its roots down in certain places. Maybe not roots. More like a cell tower. So he, Potentially Patrick, is drawn into this place. Orns–Obs–Ossory. Yes. That's it.

"He makes camp for the night. At first there's nothing going on but he wakes up to these whispers in the dark. Calling his name, sounding like his friends. Out of the shadows comes an enormous wolf and it speaks like a human. He tells Patrick to not be afraid and that he's from a clan that was cursed some years before by a real piece of work. Some druid or some such with a name like Natalis. The wolf says that, every seven years, two of their clan had to take on the skin of wolves and go live in the forest. At the end of the seven years, they return to their clan as humans again. Another two lots are drawn and those picked are next to put on the skins.

"Well, it so happened that the most recent duo were an old husband and wife. Forest life didn't agree with them and the wolf that was talking to Patrick was the old man. He explained that his wife had gotten ill and was probably going to die. So what was the old man to do? He'd gone out in search of help, only to stumble upon the priest. He asks Patrick to come with him and administer the Holy Sacrament. That's when you do the last rites and take the body and blood of Jesus on your deathbed...These damn things always asking for human flesh, ain't they?

"Well, the priest didn't have much choice. Saving a cursed being from certain damnation? That's a fine feather in your cap. Patrick went with the wolf into the woods, and there at the foot of a great tree, lay the bitch. Obviously close to death. Patrick approached her and asked if there was some sort of proof she was an old woman and not a savage thing ready to rip off his face. The old man wolf said that if Patrick cut open part of the skin, he'd have all the proof he needed. Patrick took a knife out of his camping kit, slit open the belly and wouldn't you believe! The face of a shrivelled old woman stared back at him.

"When he realised that he wasn't being tricked by all manner of hodags that slink around the far corners of the woods, Patrick performed the last rites and sent her soul off to heaven. Patrick returned to his bishop. The bishop had this Gerald of Wales fellow write up a report and send it to the pope. I can't say if the pope actually read any of it, but it shows how serious the matter is. The idea is, if God made man in His own image, and man is able to transform his soul into a beast or tree or rock or even another person! You know what that means?" She doesn't wait for me to reply but ploughs on. "It means that the wall between the earthly and the divine crumbles. Then what?"

"So the thing outside," I ask, unsteady in trying to keep up with the flood of information. "It's a werewolf?"

Mama rolls her wild, wide eyes. "You aren't listening! It doesn't become another. It takes! It takes the skin of a living thing and since any living thing is of God, It is God. But It's also cursed, driven by the base needs of desire and the need to keep a fresh skin. There's more than movie monsters and your daddy's fairy stories out in the world, little girl."

"S-s-so. What do we do?" I can't believe this is a real conversation we're having. It makes no sense! It's the drivel of an insane person. "Do you have a priest on speed dial?"

Mama slings a roll of bubble wrap at me. I duck and it careens off the empty wall behind me. "How *dare* you!" It's the first time she's raised her voice at me. I scramble for safety but I'm trapped against the sofa. Mama stands, ash tumbling from her housecoat as she slams one fist into an open palm. "You brought Its attention! You called It to this house! You are responsible! The least you could do is take this seriously. You filthy, rotten child!"

With each statement her body expands and stretches until she is a black, quilted cloud hovering over me. I shrink into the cushions, unable to do more than tremble. The hard, sweet scent of Karo syrup and nicotine of her breath plumes against my face. She absorbs me, chokes me with her eyes, and it's like the house is crumbling into her vortex.

"Let me fix it! I can fix it!" I plead, head turned and arms slung over my face as though it's enough to protect me from whatever she's prepared to throw at me next. Hands. Axe. Teeth. "I can make it better! I promise!"

The air snuffs out and, when I open my eyes, Mama's sitting in her chair again, like she's not moved at all. "And what do you do when you promise?"

I sit up, wipe the snot and saliva from running down my cheek and neck. Unable to look at her, I twist the blue cotton of my nightgown between shaking fingers and whisper, "I keep it."

Chapter Nine

Rash promises always come with steep consequences. People make and break promises all the time: to stones, animals, lovers, children, themselves and, inevitably, those promises always get broken. That's why Mama and Daddy always taught me to not make one unless I know, without a doubt, that I'm able to honour one. In real life, nothing happens if you break it. Sure, you might hurt feelings, and maybe there's a financial loss to go with it, too, but it's not life ending. If you fail, the world doesn't stop spinning and decide to plummet itself headlong into the sun's fiery centre.

Fairy tales are another matter entirely. That's why they're called *rash* promises. When something goes wrong or you get a little feckless and self-centred about the whole issue, the moment you don't think the rules apply to you, the bad happens. All manner of trouble from inconvenient to fatal comes in the result of a promise made too quick. The rashness of it prickles and itches and flakes until everyone can see you're an unreliable failure. So you've got to keep the promise or your skin rots and falls off. You get bad luck. Your wife ends up with a sausage stuck under her nose. Your mother will kill you.

I know this the same way I know my hair is short and

brown without having to look in the mirror. I guess that means some of what Daddy tried to teach me did stick, contrary to Mama's opinion.

There's an oddness about the way Mama doesn't move. She's a snake coiled up and waiting for me to expose an ankle. Stupid me, thinking I knew how to hold a snake, thinking we could be a family. A normal, honest to God, best-friends-with-my-mother family.

"So. What do I do?"

She clicks her tongue. "You made a promise but don't know how to fulfil it? Of course." With another series of grumbles, Mama gets to her feet. "We wait It out. Hopefully the wards will hold." Then she shuffles out of the living room, clutching her black housecoat between her arthritic, red tipped fingers, like it's a loose elephant skin trying to slosh off.

"Where are you going?"

She stops, half turns to look at me, and a weird combination of disgust and resignation ripples the wrinkles on her cheeks. "I'm going to get a new box of cigarettes. Want me to tell you if I have to take a piss?"

"No," I whisper.

She pats my hand, like she knows I'm scared, but she leaves me regardless. Her skin is the wrong kind of cold and it leaves a trail of ice on my veins. What's worse? Stuck inside a house with a killer or take my chances with the thing outside? If she was a good mother, she would have held me tight. Aunt Lou clung to me so hard the night I moved in with her I nearly suffocated in her Burberry perfume.

Ignoring the panicked *thud-thunk* between my ears, I listen for the floorboards above to creak. Mama moving around, searching for her Virginia Slims, acting as though this is the most normal thing in the world. Now is my chance!

Using the lamplight as far as it will reach, then the walls to guide me, I worm my way down the dark hall and back into my room. My cheap leather purse hangs from the daybed post and I grab it, not bothering with shoes or a coat. That can all be replaced. It's the car keys I need. They're not on the tassel hook but they're not on my nightstand. It takes a moment to find them at the bottom of the bag, sliding under all the gum and cough drop wrappers. With the keys in my hand, poised and ready between my knuckles like tiny daggers, I'm on the move.

The house is alive and shudders with our tandem steps. Mama upstairs. Me down. I try to move to her rhythm so she can't hear me but there's no masking the heavy screech of the door as I swing it open, nor the thudding of my feet, louder than it is in my ears, as I sprint down the porch and towards the Avalon. It isn't far. It shouldn't be. I parked in front of the house. Directly in front of, so why is it down the driveway? Why is it getting further from me? The threat of something charging me, that *thing*, coming from the trees.

I slam against the front passenger door. A bloodletting howl pierces the pounding in my ears. My hands rattle, uncontrolled. Stupid! Stupid hands! They're so sweaty it's hard to grasp the keys as they scrape against the door handle. Finally, I shove it into the lock and fling myself into the car but something yanks at my feet.

The wet, slick growl of a predator heats against my skin, burning holes down to the bone with each droplet of saliva. My heel connects with something hard as I kick out, refusing to tear my eyes away from the steering wheel. Key in the ignition but my lower half is yanked and I can feel my spine detaching. I'm nothing more than a dirty sock for the dog to play with. I scream a warning, kick again, slam the gears into drive. I don't stop kicking until the pressure comes off my ankle. There's another staggering howl, but it's distant.

The crunch of gravel under the car is drowned out by my own body dragging against the earth. Using the steering wheel and armrest to hoist myself into the Avalon, I beg for it to gain speed down the hill. *Please! Please! Go!* I can't move out of the passenger seat, my entire body vibrates so terribly that I can't control the limbs or my breathing. My vision prickles at the corners, all black fuzz and deep water. Blood drips down my legs from massive puncture wounds. Teeth or claw is uncertain but the deep red of me pools between my grass-stained socks.

An enormous shadow jumps in front of the Avalon. My ragdoll body flops against the dashboard and a flash of rotten ivory catches the moonlight, fragmented in the broken windshield. Steam hisses out of the hood of the car, hiding the shape as it comes toward me. I slam the passenger door shut and lock the doors. Like that's going to do anything to a cursed god.

The Avalon rocks back and forth, grinding against itself. Steam continues to tumble out of the hood and a new hiss of leaking fluid and air from the tires joins them. The thing is crawling onto the hood. It's toying with me. A purr of pleasure rumbles through the metal frame as I'm rocked back and forth. A gift on Christmas day. Any minute It's going to get bored with playing and smash through the frail barriers. This is not where I'd imagined dying. I always thought death would come in my sleep. Either that or in the middle of a tandem parachute jump with a completely gorgeous boyfriend who was always begging me to try new adventures with him.

"I can't die this way." The words slip out of my mouth before I realised I said them and it creates a stillness between me and the creature. Unsure if it's waiting for me to make the next move, or if it works on sound alone and I've just given myself away, I turn frantically in my seat. The pain can be ignored as long as I can keep going, keep moving, keep living. I search for anything that I can use as a weapon. An umbrella or a funny stick I picked up on a weekend hike. The only thing I have is the cigar lighter receptacle. The Avalon is old enough that there's actually a lighter inside the metal tube and not a charger for a cellphone. If that's all I have? Well, I'll take it.

I punch it into the outlet and hold tight onto the armrests, forcing myself to not scream but keep my eyes open, so I know where this creature is.

It is carved out and grizzled as the rotten corpse of a dog that crawled under the house and left too long. There's more strange shapes warped by the smoke, bent as though body parts were put on backwards, but I can't see it through the steam and nearly blinding panic. The weight of this thing crushes the windscreen and the roof of the car. The smoke coming out of the hood turns black.

Move! Get out! Run!

Where can I go except back to the house? Dead here. Dead there. I'm a field mouse that's trapped itself in the corner.

No! The forest. Get lost in the trees, lose your scent in the river. Go!

The doors are all wedged shut, dented and broken from the monster smashing the sides with its long, swooping limbs. The only way out is through the cracked windscreen. My legs are already bleeding but my heart clutches again. I'm frozen

by the idea that I'll end up lacerating myself before I have a
chance for freedom. I begin rocking with the car, using it to
propel me forward.

Bang!

My bare feet against the glass.

Bang!

The weakest parts where it's already webbing.

Bang!

A hairy, humanoid hand punches back. Tiny pebbles of
glass and thick shards spray everywhere, followed by a plume
of acrid black smoke. There's no time. The Avalon is going to
blow. I dodge, sliding into the footwell of the passenger seat.
Another vicious swipe cuts through the choked air and I grab
the cigar lighter receptacle, press hard with my thumb and
bury it into the thick fur. The monster's leathery fingers twitch
and, above me; an agonising wail is loud enough to shatter
what remains of the glass. I swallow the stink of burned,
mouldy fur, gas and smog.

The monster leaps from the roof of the car with such force
that it rolls onto its side. It skids a few feet, leaving a trail
of flames in the glass. The world spins in pale moon blues
and harsh reds. The little bit of Karo drenched pancake roll
around my guts and burns to the top of my sinuses. It all
comes spewing out of my nose and mouth.

When it finally stops, I scramble out of the windscreen
and faceplant into the cold, soft earth. Then I run. Faster and
harder than my lungs and bleeding legs have to offer. The
creature trails after, in a berserker fury. The ground pulses as I
zigzag up the hill. Icy pangs threaten to seize my muscles. The
thing behind me should be faster than me. I don't know how I
know this, but I do. It's still toying with me, herding me into

the woods. But I have to. Even if I wanted to, I'm too far away from the house.

Bramble digs into the open sores on my feet, sucking my blood in like fresh rain. Long, spindly branches grab and pull. Strands of my hair and threads of my nightgown get tangled in the trees.

Darcy! The woods whisper. The monster in the shadows calls to me too. *Come this way. Come! Follow. This way! Darcy! It's safe here in the deep.*

Chapter Ten

Sticks and sweet gum pods that hide in the spongy, damp grass pierce through my socks. I'm not sure if serpentine running works on anything but crocodiles, but it's better than rolling my ankle on something that fell out of a tree. Besides, crocodiles are ancient and so are gods. The constant zigzag disorientates me. Low hanging branches whip across my skin, pulling me one way and then another, until I'm not sure where the house sits. The mist wavers and breathes in tandem with my aching lungs. White spots cloud my vision. The industrial stink of gas and smoke burns inside my nostrils.

Please, Gagandeep! My thoughts spin outward like ivy on an unseen plane. Why do I want for him? Some deep need to be swept up and coddled in strong arms. I need someone more capable than me. A soft someone. A good someone. *Please! See the fire! Help me!*

At this point, trying to manifest help by thought projecting is no more insane than believing that a rabid, eighteen-foot, evil creature is chasing after me. I'm not even sure how tall it is, and there were only flashes of Its shape as it toyed with me in the car but it feels that way. Bigger even. All encompassing, like Its shadow alone is enough to devour me and the entire hillside. So I run. I only have myself. I *need* to depend on the strength of my own body and what it is capable of.

I don't stop until my scrawny knees buckle and I tumble into a rocky enclave near the property line. There's hardly a chance to inhale before moss covered limestone crumbles and sends me plummeting several feet. I hit the water with a hard smack; its icy fingers fan up and arrest me. The sky wavers and. for a moment, it looks as though the spindly branches of these wild trees are anchored to the stars before I realise I'm flat on my back beneath the stream's surface.

Please. Let me die.

But just as I can't rely on Gagandeep to rescue me, I can't rely on Death either. My head breaks through and I have to fight against river ivy to roll over and vomit the water I've swallowed. When I finish, I crawl to the edge and collapse into the dirt. Grime, dead leaves and blood cover my face and hands. Cold air stings into the puncture wounds on my calves. My nightgown is heavy with the brackish sting of winter water and, in the heart of the false dawn, it illuminates my location.

Let me sink into the ground. Let me be invisible.

Above, the rustle of feathers and leaves that remain in the cedar and oak surrounding the river. Somehow I've made it to my destination. Hoping it has soaked up my scent, I remain cemented to the undergrowth. If the creature finds me now, there's not a chance in the world that I can muster the energy to keep running. I lay here, knowing that I'm already dead.

Let It be quick.

Nothing. With trembling caution, I push myself into a seated position and wipe my face clean with the bottom of my skirt. There must be owls and crows above me, wood mice and skunks around me, waiting for me to move. Above, the stars spiral and splash, as though Coyote had just shaken them loose from a stolen blanket.

It's not that I *want* to die. I've never considered suicide, not even in those thought exercises at sleepovers, where someone inevitably asks what dying must feel like. Still, I know it was a mistake to try and escape in my car. The only outcome was to make me wish for a swift death. Now, for the first time, I wonder if this is how Daddy felt in his final moments.

The ringing in my ears is like one thousand tiny voices calling to me. *Darcy! Darcy! This way…*When I sit up, the pitch grows higher until it's one monotone squeal. My vision swims back into focus. Little dots of white trail around the sides, like glow worms falling from the trees. Worried that my movements might cause too much attention, I hug my knees and search for movement in the trees, then roll shaking hands down my calves to explore the damage. Tacky blood and dirt fills the grooves of my fingertips. The divots made by the monster's bite are deep and threaten to suction my touch down to the first knuckle.

My feet, raw and blue-white, catch the last of the moon as it dips between the cracks in the trees. The second smallest toe on my left is turned on its side. A strange sensation rattles in my lungs, not quite a sickness and not quite detachment, like I'm *other*. Outside myself. There's no pain and I'm not sure if it's because the bone is still under the skin. Do I shove it back into place? Or do I leave it?

Uncertain of what either decision will result in, I push onto my feet. Nauseous and staggering, the pain doesn't work its way into my brain. I sit back down again. Clearly I have a concussion that's taking full attention. As far as everything else, I'm helpless about what to do. So, I wiggle my butt down to the river and rinse the blood off my legs. I read somewhere, or maybe I watched it on a Discovery show, that it's best to pack wounds with mud. I'm not sure if it's better to do it with dry stuff because it will have less parasites in it. Or something? I don't know. At this point, I'm delirious in my confusion. So I stretch out my washed leg, pimply and frozen from the water, and just slop a bunch of mud all over the skin. Then I wiggle backward and search for a few twigs I can wrap around my feet. I use the lace from the sleeve of my nightgown to tie everything together. Time is limited. I know this, and yet, I'm grateful the monster has ended its pursuit of me. It crosses my mind that it might be allowing me to stitch myself together, in the same way it toyed with me in the Avalon. Now's not the time to be mad about that. All I can focus on is getting myself together enough to survive.

I'm being too loud. The dead leaves and twigs keep shhhh-swishing with each movement, and when I step into the shallow, frigid water, it splashes all the way up to my knees. Each lopsided footstep gives an echoing slosh. Loud enough to freeze my pulse. Big enough to force an owl out of the trees.

Promises to keep. Miles to go before I sleep.

Someone wrote that but I can't remember. In track and field, the coach teaches us to keep a cadence and a phrase with an uneven number of syllables to keep your rhythm fast. I keep the phrase on repeat in my head as I keep my eyes sweeping for jagged rocks and lurking shadows.

After a few minutes of slogging, the pressure of the water starts to highlight the pain in my toe. It starts as an itch around the makeshift splint. Then it's like a stone was implanted beneath the skin and every step pushes it in a little further.

I have to stop and figure out where I'm going. My breath

keeps catching between the frigid air and fear, turning my ribs into daggers, threatening to puncture a lung. The nearest river rock becomes my perch. I draw my knees to my chin and gulp down the urge to cry. Survive first. Feel bad later. It'll be my reward for seeing the sunlight. I keep telling myself this while I wring out the excess water from my nightgown. It's got to be close now. Swaths of blue-grey are visible through oak and cedar trees.

The moon shifts behind me and I can't smell burning plastic or gasoline. It's good that it didn't start a grass fire. One less thing to deal with.

First, I have to beat down this desperate, niggling voice that wants me to be snuffed out. Second, I *must* return to the house. Mama will be furious but fighting off an old woman has got to be safer than trying to dodge this monster forever in the woods. I convince myself that my fight will end by sunrise. All the monster movies end with everything better in the daylight.

"Miles to go," I whisper.

Generations of people survived the wilds. The rules are always stick to the path and never talk to the wolves. I can do this. I am the woods and the woods are me. This has always been my home. My heart is rooted to this earth and I'll move forward, like one of those enormous Joshua Trees migrating to their final resting place. I will not be swayed. I will not let anything chop me down. I am made to live.

Chapter Eleven

Out of all the creepy crawlies, broken bones and spindly plants I've come to anticipate on my trek back, the last thing I expected were the wild boars. The uneven, deeply rutted ground should have warned me, but I thought it was my broken toe and concussion pushing everything sideways. It takes a few minutes for the iridescent glow of the sounder's gaze to fall onto me.

The deep, rasping grunts from the elder sow spreads through the others, and their breath rises like mist off the meadow by my high school's track ring. It's deeply haunting and I have time enough to think of the thin veils that separate this human world and the supernatural one Daddy used to tell stories about. "They're old gods, come to watch us and only reveal themselves to worthy opponents."

That information is all well and good when the blankets are pulled to my ears and the nightlight is on. Now, it just sends an added shiver down my spine. I move backward with a possessed slowness. My knees and the palms of my hands are scraped by exposed roots as they sink into the mud. One by one, elongated heads pop up from the mounds. Snouts and tusks drip with sod, slime and blood. Their grunting intensifies.

The old sow steps forward, cloven hoof overgrown into sharp points. It spreads out as she steps forward, sending bubbles of liquid up from the ground. A length of deer intestine trails from her teeth. I continue to back away, not too fast to incite a riot. No joy. The rest of the sounder is moving too. The time for no sudden movements has passed. Yet again, I'm slinging myself to my feet and sprinting into the dark.

The ground thunders as rock and twig are trampled beneath them as they chase me back the way I came. Their squealing drowns out my own haggard breath. Pushing through the throbbing pain in my legs, from the broken toe and the puncture wounds, I launch into the nearest tree that looks like something I can climb.

The lowest branch is a little more than six feet off the ground. I manage to use my working toes to grip the bark to shimmy up to it. The boars screech, pushing against the trunk, jumping at my slipping feet. My arms aren't strong enough to hold me and I'm too scared to try to swing my legs up to the branch. I've never been a gym person and the unused core muscles are panicking along with me. How? How can we do the impossible?

I swing and my foot with the broken toe knocks against the rough head of a sow. She and I both scream. I managed to not fall and another boar takes her place. They try to bite at my gown but I've managed to hug the bottom of the branch like a sloth. The boars continue to launch themselves at me and the trunk. Post oaks are not big and this one sways with all the strength of a blade of grass as the boars smack their winter-thick bodies against the base. They're so frantic in their desire to devour me, they leave behind tufts of wiry brown hair and gouges from their tusks in the mossy bark.

With a grunt, I turn my body to the top of the branch. Now that I no longer have to fight myself against gravity, I can figure out how long I have before the tree falls. I inchworm back to the trunk. The branch above me is much closer and there's a knob I can use for a foothold.

I've only just braved a standing position when an ominous groan cuts through the boars' frantic gnashing and tearing. The post oak tilts, wavers at an angle, then crashes against another. The side of my face cracks against this new tree. I scramble to it before the other slides down its side, taking old branches and bark with it. The boars use it as a bridge to me but then they stop. They stare up, frenzy subdued by some other malicious force. Hugging the new tree, I risk looking down at them. Vertigo spins me and so I cling tighter to the post oak, praying it's stronger than the last.

The boars look up at me. Grizzled, slick with mud and blood. Maggots fall from their mouths and bits of meat are wedged between broken teeth. One by one, they step backward, heads swaying with their little tails. They are silent as they slip back into the shadows. I watch them, waiting. Something scared them off. I don't need the prickling skin along my arms and the back of my neck to tell me this. As my vision begins to focus, I wonder if I'll see the thing that's hunting me. Will the attention stay on the boars, giving me a chance to make an escape?

What comes out of the shadows isn't the monster. A pale, milky light filters through the dying leaves. It dapples the ground, which is not grass but bone. Bone and rot, piled into mounds. The wind shakes torn, leathery skin, bits of cloth. Hair that birds have not stolen for nests. A jumble of remains in an open grave. I gag and shut my eyes against the wretched view. At least it's almost too cold to smell the worst of the rot.

The graveyard below continues to wait for me to fall into its scavenged arms. Shaking, I move around the trunk. My knees and palms press so tightly to the bark bits of raw skin scrape off. *Be like a squirrel*, I tell myself. They do it so easy, bounding from branch to branch, faith in themselves that they won't fall. I make it to the north side of the tree. Deep green moss tickles my cheek and nose. Then it's a slow walk of the plank from one branch to the next. Smaller branches and browning leaves threaten to trip me. I hug the next tree when I get to it.

The process repeats until I've lost count of trees and the grey light slants through the trees. Out to the east, the sun, swathed in cloud, looks like a hard-boiled egg. All white, no yellow. The ground beneath has lost all its brown. Fog rolls in. From the river. From somewhere else that seems almost ungodly. It's fast as an open container of dry ice. I think I've made it beyond the bones but inhale deeply, searching for the faint and sticky scent of rancid meat. Squinting through the fog is no help. I might as well have climbed the Himalayas and lost myself in a cloudbank. Hell, I'm even walking over a mass of bones just like those explorers.

Still, it's taken me too long keeping in the trees. I should have dropped down a long time ago but the boars scared me more than the bodies. Then there was the monster; the idea of it was ever present and I didn't know if It could climb trees. I wasn't safe up here. The branches were proving increasingly difficult and I know I'll eventually fall. My legs are shaking but not from fear. I'm not sure how much longer they can hold me. The wounds have been weeping for a while now and mud is trailing down my leg, leaving a trail of any carnivore intent on taking me down. Somewhere along the way, I lost the pathetic attempt of a toe splint.

The fog continues to thicken but there's nothing moving below. There can't be. Otherwise it would start swirling in other directions…wouldn't it? I remind myself that I made it this far. No clue why, but I did. Knowing that I made it this far, it meant there was a chance I could make it all the way. My mother's house, with the sigils cut into the door, was the goal.

I drop awkwardly into the leaf-strewn grass. The landing is awkward and I pedal backward, tripping over exposed roots. It isn't long before I fall flat onto my backside, fog swirling around in wayward curls.

The silence of predawn is ending and there's a soft murmur of birds and squirrels chittering above me. They were quiet long enough to see if I survived my fall, then picked back up again. Whispers, muffled by the fog. *Darcy. Darcy.*

"Mama?" I lick my cracked lips.

Darcy! She calls again. It's her. Again and again, she calls out to me. Come home to me!

I stagger to my feet, using an unseen trunk to hoist me up. Where do I turn? The fog is so dense it's almost solid. I wave my arms frantically in a desperate bid to swim through it.

This way!

"Mama!" My voice squeaks and rasps. The fog is relentless. I keep stumbling toward where I think I hear her calling from but each step turns me around and Mama's voice ends up behind me.

Darcy! Darcy! Her calls become more frantic. Then it turns into a bloodcurdling shriek that echoes into the woods. Everything goes quiet.

"Mama!" I keep running, tripping every few feet. The inside of my mouth turns gummy and spit crusts at the corners of my mouth. Snot drips. All the water is draining from me; I'm turning into a shrivelled husk. Just when I think I can't go any further, my feet crunch against a dry patch of undergrowth and the fog lifts. It peels away, drowsy and unsure. Now I can see where I'm walking.

Now I can see, I've stepped into the bone pit.

My breath catches, the scream clutched inside my parched throat. A grizzled finger taps against the puncture wound of my leg, as if searching for blood to bring it back to life. I turn on my heels and sprint back through the forest, using the tree the boars felled. The ever present fog rolls and then lingers, then rolls again. I crash into the freezing river, palms and knees smacking hard against the water smooth stones. Half laughing, half crying, I scoop the water into my face and drink some. If I survive all this, I can worry about spores or parasites later. Thirst quenched, some of my head screws back into place.

I've realised now that Mama wasn't calling out to me. She'd still be in the house, not idiot enough to chase after me when that monster was skulking around her property. The fog confused me and the voice I heard was mimicry. Daddy used to tell me how the Green Folk liked to use familiar voices and trick people to trap them in the woods. Daddy was trying to tell me that we lived alongside danger in a way that my young heart could understand. I took for granted his yammering and countless stories. If I had listened better, what Mama was trying to say would have been clear to me. I wouldn't be lost in the forest. If I actually paid attention to all that Daddy spoke of, I don't think I would've come back.

Whispers continue to shoot through the fog like sharp daggers. Trees creak and moan, leaning in the direction they want me to go. Each points me in the opposite direction of the other. I tried going by the moss. It's supposed to grow on the north side but the bark is either clean of all moss or it's covered entirely.

I follow the river as long as it takes me. Like in the old bible stories, or the worst fairytales, the sun suspends itself on the eastern side. Time hangs itself and it's only my own heartbeat keeping the seconds ticking. Mud sloshes around my toes and I stop, muscles familiar with this place, even though I don't. The fog drifts upward and down again, revealing thin strips of rocky hills.

Several squirrels dart from the branches and into the ruts left by the wild boars, searching for what remains of their stored food. It's their swift movements and angry chitters that frighten me, so much like the whispers that have plagued me through the night. It's not as big as it felt when I fell down it but I still need to pause and catch my breath. The skin around the wounds itch terribly and I scrape off the drying mud. Then I begin my slow climb upward. It's steep enough that my knees burn and I have to fall forward to use my hands to keep me moving upward instead of back. A murder of crows' laughter mixes in with the squirrels clacking their teeth and the fog has turned to a proper mist. It drags my hair across my face in several thin snakes.

It's not long before I have to lean against a cedar to catch my breath. It juts out of the rockface, half its branches curled under as if pulled by some animal. To be safe, I check inside the shallow cave the dead branches are hiding. No snake eggs. No angry fox hissing at me to stay away from the kits. My breathing is stitched and escapes in short bursts of cloud. Everything hurts and the damp air trickles down to the bone. The skin around my broken toe is blushing red and the toenail looks ready to rot off. If I make it out alive, I'm going to join a gym. *Not if. When. When I make it out of this…*

Overhead limestone breaks and bounces down the hillside. I catch my breath and snap my head upward. I was expecting to come face-to-face with a giant, rotting claws reaching out to me. Instead I meet the golden, slanted eyes of a massive Catalina goat. Its pale beige horns jut out of a shaggy roan skull, turning outward like the sides of a square. The beard is darker and hangs from chin to forelegs. Moss and twigs dangle from the scraggly hair. The way it looks down at me is filled with utter misery, like the whole of the universe is trapped in its golden eye and all it has to do is blink and end all of Creation. With one more shake of its head, the goat leaps forward, rocks crumbling beneath its hooves.

I blink and it disappears into the mist like a phantom. I don't want to look back down the hill. I don't need to know what scared it off because I can smell the rotting, rancid breath smoking its way upward. With my head tilted toward my destination, my eyes flit to the corners as the ground rumbles and cracks below. The creature, the thing I am not brave enough to look at directly, is climbing. One thunderous claw after another. I used to watch nature documentaries to help me go to sleep and in them, the slow and thoughtful narrator always warns to never turn your back on a prowling animal.

But what choice do I have?

Before I even had a chance to scramble up the rest of the hill, the monster launched itself on top of me. With a shriek, I bury my face into the wet grass and let go. The air slices above my head as I slide back down the hill. A disturbing and grizzly howl thunders through the dawn. All the crows stop laughing and take flight. The rocks and grass nick my face and arms, leaving a trail of blood as I fall. I land flat on my back, the wind knocking free of my lungs. For a minute, all I can do is exhale in rasping gasps. Vision swimming, my eyes roll back up the hill and I'm seeing the monster fully.

It has the body of a hyena but has the thick, gnarled hands and feet of an old man. Enormous antlers protrude from its forehead but its face is elongated, canine, mostly bone held together by slick, dripping sinew. Another howl erupts. It's hollow and desperate, the way elk sound when they're shot; like the Nazgul.

I swallow my tongue, gagging on how it's swelled, and taste the blood from where I've bitten down. I roll onto my side, gagging, black specks dotting the corner of my eyes. No matter how much I want to inhale, I can't breathe. My brain is squeezed by a vice clamp. The creature turns its head toward me, and each bone click-clacks like the seconds of a windup clock. Unable to scream, I hiccup instead. That helps correct my breathing and I gulp down the sweet mossy air. There's no time to appreciate this because the monster is galloping toward me. I scramble to my feet, filling my lungs as I sprint back down the river. Mud and water splash around me. This night is unending. I'm back where I started, doomed to repeat these steps again and again. I have to break the cycle. I can't keep running but I can't let this thing snatch me either.

It isn't long before my body gives out on me and I tumble into the bank of the river. Grit fills my mouth and nose. The monster is on top of me, yanking my shoulder. I roll in the direction it's dragging me and spit all the sludge into its face. The monster releases me to clutch its skull and I kick into the concave diaphragm and it rears back with another, metal-on-metal screech. I roll out from under it then begin sprinting upward, feeling the vibrations underneath me as it slams back into the ground.

The fog swallows me whole but I keep climbing, trying to remember to go in a zigzag pattern, with no idea if it actually helps. Nothing looks familiar and the shape of the rocks and cedars all look the same. Thorns pierce the softest parts between my toes and fingers. Every minute that passes, I'm losing distance between me and the monster. Its hot, rancid breath is on my back and there are times when it runs over me, ungangly, disjointed legs passing on either side of me. The barrel chest of its body casts a shadow across me. Then it lags. Toying with me. Swatting at me. Laughing at me.

At last, I burst through the treeline. The house isn't far. The old picket fence shines in the gloomy dawn but the monster leaps, putting itself between me and the house. I skid to a half-stop and yelp as the joint in my knee pinches at the sudden turn. Blood and slime drip from the fangs protruding from the exposed jaw. Its heavy breath comes out of the wet nostrils and it stalks toward me.

"Mama! Please!" I scream out. "Mama!"

The monster makes a face; I think it might be grinning. It's hard to tell in something that doesn't have lips or flesh covering the cheeks, but it makes a sound like rocks tumbling in a metal container, like it's laughing at me.

"Help!" All the screaming is pointless. There's no one to hear me but Mama and the birds that have long been scared off. "Mama! I'm here! I'm out here!"

The monster looms in front of me, stretching to great heights. The humanoid hands reach out, grasp at the air. I'm starting to think this is the last thing I'll see, but in a moment of clarity, I remember Daddy's coal burning pit. I turn, sprint towards it before the monster can divert me again. The pit is little more than a sod mound but there must be tools there. Rusty and old doesn't matter. I just need it to stab. The monster pushes me forward and I'm falling headfirst into the pit. My forehead smacks against the wall and everything snuffs out.

Chapter Twelve

He wakes at a quarter to five each morning and takes a box of matches down from the mantel to light the fire. Sometimes, all the time, he misses the luxury of electricity. Sacrifices, he learned long ago, must be saved. The plugs in the walls and the empty light bulb sockets are covered in cobwebs. Each morning, while the coffee is brewing, he dusts them clear, a little nod of hope that one day he'll be able to use modern technology again.

Once the fire is lit, he sits in his wooden chair, the one he made to rock his daughter in once she was born, and begins to grind the coffee. It's at this time, when he is alone with duties, that he doesn't talk. He rests his brain. He thinks of nothing but lighting the fire, grinding the coffee and setting it to boil, dusting the cobwebs. He listens to the movements of the birds and the way the trees speak to each other whenever the wind changes direction. People always think the country is too quiet, but he knows better. It's not the same type of loud as the city, but it moves and crawls with a rhythm of its own. The only time the countryside becomes truly silent is when he begins to worry. So, in the mornings, he does what he needs to and keeps his brain still. And he listens.

Yesterday was quiet. Today, the larks don't sing. The acorns refuse to fall from the oaks. He doesn't hear the neighbor's roosters crow. He knows today he must bring down the axe, walk into the woods and stray from the path.

At first light, his wife comes down. She leans over him and kisses the part in his hair. He loves when she is tender. He loves that she is hard, too, but that's what makes the tenderness so special. He wants to tell her all his thoughts, as though his dreams had taken him on an Odyssey and he wants to explore each minute detail with her. But she likes the quiet and he fights to keep his tongue.

She takes the kerosene lamp from the coffee table and uses it to light a Virginia Slim, then disappears into the kitchen to slice up fruit. Even though she's kissed him, he knows she's frosty from their argument the night before. She likes to start fights when he's making love to her. Never before. Never after. Right at the peak of things.

He wants to teach their daughter the way of his people. It's a dying tradition, true, but a vital one. All this time, he's guided her thoughts through the stories he knows, pushing her little head to start thinking about truth and the dangers of the woods. His wife doesn't want this, however. She wants their daughter to remain ignorant, like most people, to not be swayed into this precarious and solitary life that was forced upon them. He knows his wife is still angry by the way she handles the knife. A dull thud after each crisp slice, filling the gaps of silence between them.

He brings his coffee cup to the sink and rinses out. "I go to the woods today."

"What? Already?"

"I love you. Did you know that?"

"Tell me again and I might believe it."

She puts down the knife, dripping with pink apple juice, and leans her cheek toward him. He presses his lips and stubble against her soft skin and finally gets a laugh out of her. She follows him to the front door, cupping her bony elbows in her hands, and watches with keen, dark eyes, as he disappears into the woods.

This place is as familiar to him as every single lash on his daughter's eyes. His father was a charcoal burner, and his father before him. Still, he appreciates his wife's concern. She's seen him go off the path twice before and seen him return, victorious in his troubles. When you're in love, time wiggles around like mercury in a petri dish. It's easy to not realise another seven years have passed. His wife comes from a people who never counted time by the hour or the day. If it weren't for the terrible marking of each seven-year cycle, he could tell her each month, "I go to the woods today," and she'd look up in surprise and say:

"What? Already?"

The first time, she went with him. He'd been many times before, but it was the first time since their marriage. She needed to wholly understand the task he committed to. She did well, extraordinarily. In fact, she was a natural, and he wished that it hadn't been so hard a thing for her to bear. He knows it's not for everyone. It is a difficult burden and not because it means to hunch down in the muck, waiting hours for the target to cross the hunter's path. There is a savage pleasure in this task and it is for this reason she will not go with him again. He needs to bury the goodness in him to do this the right way and she admitted to not wanting to see a stranger in her bed.

"Let me be ignorant," she whispered, arms looped around

the twisted legs of the body she helped carry back to the charcoal pit.

His wife is right about their daughter being too young this year. The next time he needs to go out, she will be. It isn't the firstborn he's supposed to pass down this knowledge to, but the child of the opposite gender. To him, this is an excellent sign. So much of old magic demands of the first child and he believes this will give her the extra strength needed to continue a dying tradition.

By midmorning, he finds the first tracks. Right on the edge of the path, a bend in the blackberry bushes indicates the massiveness of a body that's cut through. He touches the soft, wilting leaves, the snag of thin, silvery-roan hair. Kneeling, he examines the hoofprint that is not a hoofprint. It's split off into two claws like a whitetail or one of the Catalina goats that sometimes escapes the trophy hunting resort on the other side of the hill. The difference is that the hoof is not made of horn. Look closely enough and the thin grooves of knuckles can be seen in the mud. These creatures have strange, almost-hands, where the four fingers are stuck together in pairs. If it weren't for the inverted knees giving these monsters a distinct cervidae lope, he would have said their movements were apelike. Judging by the engorged knuckle indentations, he guesses that this particular monster is old and near to eighteen hands tall. He confirms this by checking the bend of the branches above, where antlers have scraped away the bark.

Old is harder to kill. Not impossible, but…

He tightens his grip on the axe and takes his feet off the path. Moccasined feet crunch softly against the fallen twigs and dead leaves. He avoids the elongated hole of a snake pit but hears the warning rattle anyway. As he goes deeper into the woods, the trees knit together, blocking out much of the sunlight. Green and grey moss speckle the red stones. Prickly pears jut out in unexpected places, chewed apart by rabbits and squirrels. For a while, he strains to hear any bird but there is only the occasional machine gun tap of a woodpecker. He stops only to drink water, refamiliarise himself with the monster's tracks and inspect the bark that flakes off the post oaks like dandruff.

He holds the axe in both hands across his chest. The handle is rubbed down smooth by decades of use. How many before him held this axe? Three or four? The silver head itself is sharpened paper fine but flecks of dried Florida water take away the shine. He stops walking well after midday. Close to the river now, it's as good a place as any to make camp. He finds the pine tree he's sat beneath so many times before, checks for any sign of a new critter moving in, then shifts the fallen red nettles around into a comfortable pile. The goal isn't to make a secure and well-hidden camp. He needs to be smelt and seen. After all, he has what the monster wants, so the goal is simply to wait out the creature in an area he feels he has the upper hand.

This is the lowest part of the creek. Further north, the land spikes into sharp, unpredictable ridges and he's too heavy to trust the thinner points of limestone. He makes charcoal to pay the bills and he uses the water from the river to make mud for the mound where he burns the wood. It yields better results than the water from the well and, anyway, that's used by everyone in the town. There have been too many dry days for him to be lazy and use the tap water.

When he gathers water, he likes to eat the lunch his wife makes. Usually it's fat pasties with golden, flaky dough. The right side has a shepherd's pie filling, and the left is something sweet. Sometimes spiced apples. Sometimes blackberry compote. When she's not feeling well, he makes himself a tin of soup and carries it in a long, thin Thermos. He doesn't eat when it's time to hunt. The task, no matter how many times he's done it, makes him a little queasy. Maybe because he knows what's at stake. He's seen the monster at work, the way it flays apart new skin with the thin edges of its long, acidic tongue. He's seen the monster slide, bone crackling, into a fresh body. It doesn't take much for him to imagine how it would feel to have his skin peeled off of him while still breathing. His wife knows when he dreams of these things because he goes off meat for a few weeks afterward. Even when he tries to hide it, she can see it in the paling pink of his eyelids. She pulls them down to check him at least once a month.

"You need iron," she says, then he'll eat meat again.

He doesn't sleep. These monsters move in the shadow and prefer the dark but that's not a dependable piece of information. On more than one occasion, he's seen one walking through the fields along the long stretches of highway. When they get close to populated areas like that, they're already wearing a skin. He's not sure if that's the only time they feel comfortable walking in the daylight, but he knows a hitchhiker isn't human when there is a particular shine in their eye. Pearly. Haunting. He also doesn't see the point in falling asleep at a location he selected. That would be like getting caught with his pants down.

Silence is hard for him. He understands the necessity of it, why his wife thrives in it, but knowing something doesn't automatically make things easy. He can't figure out if his daughter is more like him or more like his wife, but she doesn't

drift when he talks and that has to mean something. He
doesn't mind being solitary in the woods. Generally speaking,
it's rarely quiet. He likes to talk to the mockingbirds and the
robins. He mimics the chittering of squirrels and wood mice.
He listens to the hawks. He believes the vultures have more
to say than anyone gives credit. Skunks are as curious and
social as raccoons and, truthfully, he likes the way they smell.
It's only when a monster comes, does the earth stop moving.
Silence, truly dead silence, enters the woods. That's what's
hard for him.

Last time he was out in these woods, with this axe, he had
wondered what his last thoughts would be too. They hadn't
made any sense to him then, and they don't now, but he thinks
about it again. Just as before, a span of Milky Way is visible
through the canyon gap in the unfurling leaves. In school, he'd
been taught that those stars were already gone and what he
could see with his naked eye was a death rattle. Lately, he'd
been hearing stories about other planets and things being
captured by those fancy telescopes, and he's started to wonder
if the people on those worlds can see the spark of light that
comes from Earth. Are they seeing his death like he's seeing
theirs?

Surprisingly, it doesn't make him feel insignificant or small
to think this. He's not sure he even understands what he was
trying to say to himself, but he doesn't feel small. It makes
him feel a part of a big purpose that's winking into the great
unknown, that he's part of something seen in a million miles
of darkness.

It tires his mind to think so richly, so he murmurs stories
to himself. How Coyote made the night sky. The story of
Finn McCool pretending to be giant, hairy baby to hide from

CuChulian. The warrior brothers who all became stars, except for one, pulled down by their mother, who became a cedar tree. He knows a few Anansi tales. The dirty ones where he's always having sex with village women or stealing the balls off of Tiger. His wife likes to hear about the hooded crow who became a prince. She always tells him it feels familiar to her, like something her own mother must have told her when she was very young.

There are so many stories of stolen princes and animals, origins of rocks, stars, grass. He wonders why the animals stopped talking like people or if it was simply that people forgot how to speak like animals. When he thinks like this, he thinks of the monsters. Their strangeness and indecisive bodies. Not man. Not animal. They live in a purgatory of both and neither. He has to justify why they must be killed. A stolen life is not one worth living. The monsters know this too. That's why their skin rots away and they have to cycle through new flesh. If they were something more graceful or romantic, like a Silkie, then he might put down his axe and stop hunting them. Silkies have their own skin they covet and protect. They don't take what isn't theirs, unless it's the desperate love freely given by men who stumble upon them. This is his own story. For he had stumbled upon his wife and she gifted him a precious skin.

These monsters have nothing of their own but the greed and the curse that keeps them pushing into other bodies. He doesn't know how many are left. What about hunters like him? He's never known another but surely there are. He's read stories about monsters akin to his own, living in exotic places across the ocean. What happens when the last monster is killed? Can it happen? Should it?

At dawn, he stands and dusts his jeans. He wiggles his toes, slightly sweaty inside the worn leather of his moccasins. He bought them at a flea market for three dollars and only wears them when he needs to hunt. A few of the yellow and blue beads have fallen off the design. No doubt a bird stole it for her nest. The leather is suspect, maybe even fake, but they've held up. At least, he hasn't needed to replace the soles yet.

He twists his back, popping the stiffness out of the spine. Then he stretches his arms and shoulders, resting the axe handle across the back of his neck. His dark eyes scan upwards, searching for a physical mark to place this sudden alertness in his veins. The crows were restless and he turned his attention to the vibrations in the earth, the subtle shift of stone and grass that steered his intuition toward preparation. He didn't see the thing but he knew it was out there, hunting the hunter. The hair on the backs of his knuckles stood just as much as the ones on the nape of his neck.

At home were his wife and child, a warm spot by the fire and a meal. Maybe hot. It depended on how she felt and what time he finished this. The work is grim and he doesn't enjoy lingering in it but it isn't a job he can hurry up with either. Mistakes are the reason these monsters can get so old. It isn't a luxury that he only has to do this every seven years. That's too much time to relax, to slow down and either get too scared or too cocky. No distractions. That's what his mother taught him. Days like these, mortal pleasures are the most tempting. She told him it was part of the monsters' power to sway thoughts and focus. Personally, he thought that it would be too embarrassing to admit that his final thoughts were on food, like a glutton, and not on something more in the path of higher learning. Like his family or his purpose. So, as much as he wants to think about beans, cornbread and slices of fresh jalapeno mixed into fried chitlins, he can't.

Now is the hunting hour. These monsters walk between the wolf and the dog, when the light is at the toughest angle and confuses the shape of any living thing. Now he must depend on the spirits to guide his hand. If it's their will for him to see the next sunset, they'll help guide his hand. It's foolish for a man to think it's him and him alone that has the strength and the skill to slay a creature that is unworldly, inhuman, a god.

No one is exactly sure how old these monsters are. Somewhere down the long line of oral tradition, the information was jotted down as an incomplete truth. He thinks, although there is no one to verify this or to ask an opinion of, that these monsters are who God speaks to in the very beginning, when the Good Book reads "He turned to *Them* and said 'this is good'". No preacher he ever came across explained who or what Them were. So he can only assume they're fallen celestials, as old as when the light was separated from the darkness. Angels. Demigods. Beings that created the light long before the sun was ever dreamed up. Whatever their origins, the one fact that stays consistent throughout each telling, is this: they prey on humans. They take skin to become like man.

They can never be man because they lack the free will. So they mimic, hoping it's enough to satiate the desire. It's not and the skin sloshes off too fast for them. They hunt again. Take again. Try again. Lower themselves to be like men so they can separate themselves from an overbearing creator? Maybe. He doesn't think the Higher Powers are overbearing but perhaps that's just because he has free will and doesn't know any better.

This thought hurts his head the way thinking about the

universe does, and it derails him from focusing on the present moment.

The trees are bending sideways, leaning into the shadows, and the birds have all abandoned their nests. Rabbits and voles bound through the undergrowth, as quickly as trying to escape a forest fire. Here. Now. The monster comes.

It doesn't blend into the foliage. It doesn't move in soft measures. This is because It doesn't care if It's seen or heard by prey because nothing else is fast enough or strong enough to stop It from getting what It wants. The saplings bend and sway as the beast pushes through, following the scent. Hunter to hunter. No fear.

Except he's always afraid. He's just glad he doesn't vomit like the first time. He squares off and grounds his feet. His toes are roots spreading to the centre of the core of the earth. The axe in his hands is anointed and the silver is heavy but balanced in his big hands. *Remember, just because you cut off Its head, doesn't mean it won't bite.*

The monster bursts through, meat-rotted breath curling off of its elongated mouth in waves of smoke. Antlers, with countless points, spur and crack against the canopy. It reaches out with a massive, humanoid hand, twisted and swollen with puffy veins. Rough pads graze him. His own roots pop out of the cold ground and he bounces like a pebble into the water. Never has he seen anything this huge. More than eighteen hands.

He swallows his tongue, gags at the gritty river splashing into his mouth and up his nose. The monster leaps and slams its fingers, too long to be human, too hairless to be anything else. It digs the thick yellow nails of Its large almost-human toes into his flesh. Twigs and wet mulch fall from the wiry fur of a barrel chest the size of a family van. It leans down, shakes the skinless face into his, like It's laughing.

He swings his axe. It thumps into the convex stomach and old, blackened blood spurts from the wound as he continues to slash it upward, falling into his hair and eyes and into the water like a heavy hailstorm. The monster's hide sizzles and pops and a throaty, elklike shriek thunders through the woods. The ground rattles and shakes. Loose limestone plinks down the hills. The monster rears back, giving him a chance to scramble out from under it, to look for high ground. The deep injury isn't enough to stop It or slow It. The monster charges him, no longer playing but fully prepared for war. He feels the burn in his chest, the stings and cuts of branches that slap across bare skin as he races through the woods. His eyes spin wildly to the shadows. Where is the other one? They always come in pairs.

He's grateful to know that his breath is there, that his skin belongs to him. At first, he doesn't realise that he's hit a break in the treeline or that the sun has reached a higher point in the sky. The monster's massive shape eclipses everything. He slips in the blood saturating the browning grass as he lunges toward Its thick neck. He swings his axe with a mighty yell of his own and he prays his aim is true.

*

It's dusk on the third day when he returns home. She hears the rhythmic thump of him cleaning the muck off his boots by the door. Another as he sets his axe against the wall. She doesn't like it in the house because then their daughter will ask questions. Then she will know of the evil that engulfs their tiny home. She wants her daughter to have a few more years before she begins this uphill battle.

When he comes in, turning up the gas lamps as he moves through the hall, she waits for him to call out. She prepares herself to listen to a long-winded story about some sort of finch he saw or a rabbit dancing with the foxes. A long night of nonsense that will delight her daughter and give her fantastic, fairy-dust dreams. Instead, he greets no one and goes right to his chair by the hearth. She brings him tea.

"Did you do it?"

"I put it in the pit and burned it."

"Are you hurt?"

He hesitates and gives her an exhausted smile. "No. Only a little sore."

She sees a strangeness in the dim glow of the lamp she holds in her hand. There's something wrong with his eyes.

Chapter Thirteen

Dirt rolls around my tongue and sticks to the grooves in my molars, like I've swallowed the whole universe only to end up choking. Blinking, confused, I spread my hand out. A grub wiggles from one knuckle to the next. It burrows back into the cold ground and I inhale. Old ash, dried clay, life. I'm not sure where I am until my foot knocks against charred wood. Daddy's charcoal pit. I remember standing on the porch, bare toes hanging off the edge, watching him dig. The wood always sounded like dice rolling in a cup. Or bones. The parts that scared me the most was when he disappeared into the black mouth of it. The pit never looked man-sized from the outside but it devoured him whole when he worked to pull out each bit of charcoal. He always told me to stay back. I should have listened.

The smell of dead wood and rotten leaves mingles with the fresh dribble of blood coming out my nose. I gag as I roll sideways onto a broken rib. Tears wipe away the grime on my cheeks and I huddle here, trying to see around the small gap my body made in the side of the pit. Is it out there, waiting? Can it smell the fear drenching me? I can't see anything through the gap except the hair-fine threads of weed mixed into the mud walls and the mist that dapples the meadow between me and the house.

If only I knew where the axe was, I'd go directly toward it. Maybe Mama brought it inside when she first made sigils on the door? She would know what to do and I could dwell again on the fact that running to my car had been a huge mistake, but that wouldn't save me now.

For the first time, I feel my toe throbbing and the heat of infection in the gouges across my leg. Breathing is a shallow exercise but my lungs ache in a desperate attempt to try and catch up with me. *Where is the monster?*

There's nothing outside of the pit but the dew slick grass and a few crows hopping from the ground and into the trees. I close my eyes and envision the space between where I am to the front door. My bedroom window is closer. When I was a child, I would watch my father build the pit each season with mud and the sticks from down by the river. He filled it with logs and smoke. I remember sometimes there were clothes. When I was five, I asked him who the clothes belonged to. He told me that they were no one's. "They're infected. Remember the Velveteen Rabbit? How his little boy had to burn everything because of an illness? That's why." He said it in a way he expected me to not ask again. He had a look in his eyes that scared me, like it was inhuman.

Okay, I tell myself. *Get to the window and get inside.*

Although I allow myself another chance to breathe, I know that if I don't move soon, the few moments of safety will swiftly vanish. I pull myself into the crouch I've seen relay racers do and ignore the trembling pain in my leg. Then I count myself down. On one, I burst out of the dome. Flakes of mud and grass crumble into my hair and bounce from my nightgown to the ground. Once again I gasp for air, heart thumping in my ears. The pulse isn't loud enough to eclipse the thunder of the monster racing behind me. The huffing of Its lungs is like a charging war horse.

I want to scream for mama but all that comes out of me is a rasping, "Maaaah! Maaah!" as I desperately try to keep from tripping into my death. With a nasty splintering crack of wood and glass, I slam face-first into my bedroom windows. They warp and wiggle like all the times small sparrows have flown into them. I claw at the frames, nails breaking apart as the paint peels, but they stay tightly shut.

The whistling wind rushes over my head and I'm punted away from the window by the monster's gnarled, humanoid hands. I bounce like a flat stone on a lake. Dazed, with no time to think about where I've landed, I scramble from the tall grass to the gravel road that leads down to a smouldering Avalon.

Up! Up! Back up the hill! I know that I'll be safe once I cross the sigils cut into the porch because Mama told me I would be. If a girl can't trust her mother, then who?

Dirt and pebbles did into my skin, pockmarking every inch of me that is still alive and bleeding and hot with panic. To the right of me, the shifting blur of shadow and grizzled fur. The blinding white of skull and horn. Closing in but toying with me. Still? Vomit dribbles down my chin and I hadn't even felt the surge of my belly.

My bare feet thunder up the porch steps and the front door gives, almost as if it was waiting for me before it swung itself open. I slam it behind me and bolt the lock before my legs finally give out. The thin fabric of my nightgown bunches and snags against the sigil carved into the wood. Shaking with the raw static rolling through my veins, I bury my face into my hands. Gags and tears rattle out of my exhausted body. A warm embrace catches me off guard and I try to get back onto my feet but it's Mama. She pulls me back into her thin arms and I inhale the mix of Karo syrup and menthol Virginia Slims.

I cling to her, broken nails digging into her. She rocks me back and forth. "Shhh. I won't let go. I have you now."

"Mama! Mama!" My head throbs from all the crying and it takes more energy than I have to open my eyes. I tilt my head back to look into her eyes, dim from the windowless hall. She smooths my hair back, gently picking twigs and leaves away. Her skin is cold, the way old people get when there's not enough life in them and at the age where it shifts around in loose folds.

"It's going to be fine now." Her smile is soft, satisfied. "I've got you now."

Her hand drops away from my face and her fingers curl around mine. I look down, wanting to capture the comfort of being held by her with all my senses. On the inside of her wrist is a fresh, circular burn. A burn I put there with the cigar lighter from my car. I wriggle free but her grip is frighteningly strong. Her arthritic fingers are in bunches, like cloven hooves.

"It's alright," she repeats. "I've got you now."

Chapter Fourteen

When the sun first begins to peek through the fog, Gagandeep rubs the crust from his eyes. He is sure that he'd nodded off somewhere between three and four that morning. It isn't like he *feels* he's gone to sleep, but when the cowbell above the door clacks, he startles and there is a little bit of slime from his mouth that fell into his beard. A trucker gives him an understanding nod, grunts for the bathroom. After this, he buys a large coffee and a lukewarm samosa, then he leaves.

Gagandeep walks around the store. He sweeps, even though the floors are clean. He dusts in spite of every single can gleaming like it just came off the factory line. He switched from coffee to water. He's already had so much caffeine that his urine is dark, and his ears feel buzzy. He keeps looking at the clock but the arms never move, and Gagandeep worries that he might nod off again and he'll be too disoriented to be charming for Darcy.

Then, quite out of nowhere, it's seven in the morning and his father saunters into the store with a mug of hot tea and a newspaper tucked under his arm.

"Any business?" he asks, punching open the till. Tea and paper aside, he dumps the coin dishes onto the counter and begins to count. Mr. Kuar's beard is dark but the springy curls of moustache have all gone white.

"Nah. The Oak Farms guy that always takes the old samosas, but that's it. Oh, and Ms. Binh came right before you."

"Mm-hah. Like clockwork." He shakes his head, slides dimes into his callused hands. "Gagandeep! Where are you taking those buns?"

Gagandeep straightens from where he'd been glancing into the fresh doughnuts Ms. Binh brings every morning to help promote her business. She only brings chocolate glazed and plain crullers, preferring to keep the better options at her bakery. Gagandeep takes a square of butcher paper out of the box by the display. "I was going to bring breakfast to Mrs. Mills. Her daughter came last night to help her pack."

Mr. Kaur strokes his moustache and a frustrated sigh ripples the pale hairs. "She must be pretty. This daughter. Bring her the day-olds; we can't afford to lose money by giving away the good stuff."

Gagandeep does as asked. It's just as well. Day-old doughnuts aren't so terrible with a good cup of coffee. He does his best to arrange them so that Darcy would know that he made an effort even though he is so exhausted. Besides, she is very pretty and he wants to bring her something that is pretty too.

"You go deliver that breakfast and then you get some rest," Mr. Kaur says. He writes down numbers in a tiny notebook. "I've instructed your mother to let you be. She's agreed that your chores can be put off for tomorrow, but you must not dally with those Mills." He wags a stubby finger and then shifts his thin eyebrows. "A pretty woman is nothing if she cares not for your health!"

"No, sir," Gagandeep grins and kisses his father before leaving. "I won't dally. I'll go straight home after a simple, 'good morning!'"

"Mm-hah!" Mr. Kaur grumbles again. At last, he looks away from his mathematics and stares into his tall son's dark eyes. "I am very proud of you."

Gagandeep blushes and clears his throat. "Baba."

"See? Now you're fishing!" He claps his hand on Gagandeep's shoulder and laughs deep from his belly. The heat of his hand seeps into Gagandeep, clutching his lungs and heart. He never wants his father to let go.

The fog continues to roll in. Or is it mist? Didn't he know the difference at some point? Something to do with how far he could see into it. Or how low it sweeps against the ground. Gagandeep keeps the fog lights on and leans over the steering wheel, hoping he doesn't hit a wild boar. They like to come close to the roads when it's cold and empty. He hopes Darcy doesn't get snooty about his truck. It's not old enough to be retro but not new enough to be chic. She has an Avalon though, so hopefully that means she won't mind an old clunker pulling into the drive. Gagandeep gets to the property gate and puts his truck into park, then yanks up the parking brake.

The gate swings open with an ancient groan and leaves rust in life lines of his hands. He cradles the box under the other and hopes that when it's opened, the chocolate isn't smeared everywhere but the doughnut. As he walks up the hill, gravel crunching under the heel of his boots, shapes unfold from the mist. The fog?

At first, Gagandeep thinks it is some sort of stone for a rock garden, but as he gets closer, the lumpy shape becomes a car upended like a turtle. The weird smell is almost unnoticeable but he thinks of when he was young and pushed his coke straw into one of the votive candles his mother uses when she prays. Plastic. Wrong.

Gagandeep quickens his pace, blood in his throat. Darcy gave off the air of a city slicker. Maybe she didn't understand how to use the parking brake? Or maybe she got surprised by a boar or a whitetail?

"Hello?" he calls out, knocking on the door's frame. All the windows in the house are dark. "Mrs. Mills? Darcy? Are you okay?"

Gagandeep sets the box of doughnuts on top of the woodpile and jumps off the porch. He walks around the house, pressing his face into the windows, except the tall French style ones that are cracked. It isn't a large house and in minutes, he's back at the front.

Darcy is there, standing on the top step, lighting the lamp that hangs on a hook. "Gosh, this fog!" She smiles and tilts her head up to the bleak, muted sun. Her eyes shine. "Did you make it here okay?"

"I did," he folds his hands in front of him and shifts his feet. The gravel crunches again and again and for some reason he thinks of bones. "Are you okay? I saw what happened to your car."

"Oh?" Darcy talks in vague, slow loops like she's just woken up. Her hair is mussed and her skin is tight and shiny like a doll. She doesn't sound like the fast-witted girl who spoke with him last night, and he isn't sure if making a dirty joke would be appropriate now. Darcy's shimmering gaze turns to him. "Did something happen? I've been inside with my mama all night."

"It's flipped over," he says dumbly. How would they not hear it? "I know a guy who could tow it."

"That's so sweet of you. Yes." Darcy smiles, slow and dripping like Karo syrup. "Come inside. You can use my phone."

She turns, then glances over her shoulder to flutter her eyes at him. He likes the way she does this, all elegance and ethereal like she's about to suggest he buy a new, alluring perfume. He almost doesn't notice the pale strip of skin running down her spine. Red and white patterns thread into each other, a zipper that weeps blood and plasma. He notices that her skin doesn't fit, pulled too tight around the elbows. Through the shift of her cotton nightgown, he sees that her knees are inverted. It's as though an animal had tried to squeeze bits and pieces of her over its body. Her eyes are illuminated and her lashes flutter again. "Hey you?" she calls out to him, teasing. What sharp teeth she has. "Aren't you coming inside?"

Discover Luna Novella in our store: